SkyFire

Mike Miles

SkyFire

(Unedited - Unabridged)

For comments, copies or for more

information, contact:

Brushfire Publications

P. O. Box 777

Youngsville, LA 70592

Phone: 337-781-3280

ISBN: 978-0-578-05789-7

e-mail: brushfirepublications@yahoo.com

Dedication

"This book is dedicated to all those committed to making a difference"

About the Author

Mike Miles is someone just like you.
He listened to a still small voice one night,
got up, and started writing this book.

Acknowledgements

The first pastor who greatly influenced my spiritual foundation, Pastor R. S. King said, *"we are the sum total of all that we've been exposed to in life."* He, as well as the circle of friends and family that God has placed in my life are largely responsible for this book coming into existence.

My wife, Jerelyn, deserves as much credit, maybe even more than I do, since she so faithfully gave her support throughout this undertaking. My daughter Paula inspired me to use her name as the leading spiritual character in the story. I see her maturing into the same type of strong-willed Christian, as is the character of "Paula" in SkyFire.

Paul Atkins, the "brother I never had", has been a supportive, faithful and true friend since the day we met. Anthony C. Rock Jr. or "Rock" as he's known to all around him, has more than lived up to his namesake and has always been a consistent and positive influence in bringing the *SkyFire* story to others.

There are other *"Pauls"* and other *"rock solid"* influences in my life that are too numerous to mention here. There is someone however, who more than any other deserves all the praise, all the glory and all the honor for this book. Hopefully, you will find Him in the following pages.

Table of Contents

Table of Contents

Chapter 1

Wedding Dance

Houston, Texas

Darren Alexander hurried toward the crosswalk at about the same pace that the rush-hour traffic was running. Just as he launched out into the crosswalk, a firm hand jammed his shoulder, sending him reeling backwards a step and forcing him down to one knee. He gathered himself and looked for what he thought would be the professional football player who had just stiff-armed him. As he rose to his feet, a delivery truck careened out of control right in front of Darren. It smashed into the side of a stretch limousine gliding through the intersection. The two vehicles folded together, and the impact threw both vehicles into several parked cars nearby.

Crunching, breaking glass and screeching tires provided the soundtrack to the exploding display. Darren's analytical mind did some quick calculations and he realized he could easily have been caught in the middle of that collision had the stiff-arm assault not kept him out of the walkway. He looked around for anyone nearby who seemed capable of bringing him to his knees with one hand. There was no one. Confused, Darren watched the accident scene as people rushed in from every direction.

Sensing no need for his aid and afraid of being late on this special day, he resumed his course toward his objective. Half a block later, Darren bustled into the lobby of Houston KNOW Channel 8 Television studio stride for stride with Eddie, the night-shift copy editor. His cell phone displayed 4:21 p.m. as he veered toward the privacy of the men's restroom. He wasn't as late as he feared. Ralph, the first-floor janitor, was the only other occupant in the restroom and he was just finishing the afternoon tidy-up.

"Afternoon, Mr. Alexander," greeted Ralph.

"And to you also, Ralph," replied Darren as he stopped to straighten himself in front of the mirror. Although Darren stood over six feet, three inches tall and looked as if he might be some type of professional athlete, his only sports involvement was high school football. The slight build he was beginning to develop was more the result of over nine months of fairly regular work-outs at the local gym. Darren mussed his sandy brown hair to evoke the un-kept style of the day.

When Ralph exited the room, Darren seized the opportunity to do what he had really entered the restroom to do. He reached into his pocket and brought out a small jeweler's box. Under the artificial light of the vanity area, he opened the box. Gleaming under the multiple lights was a radiant-cut diamond, just under two carats, in a white-gold setting.

Was this the day he would come up with a clever way to ask her? Would she say yes? Would she like the ring? Where would be the best place to pop the question? Would she laugh at the whole idea and devastate his already fragile male ego? Would she walk away, her heels clicking softly on the terrazzo floor, while making a belittling comment like, "What were you thinking?"

"Terrazzo floor!" The vision of his worst fear playing out in his mind brought him to his senses and out of the mini-melodrama. The terrazzo floor! He wouldn't be proposing to her while they were in the men's restroom standing on the terrazzo floor! "Wake up, fool," he said to himself as he put the box back into the pocket of his sport coat, glanced quickly into the mirror, and resumed his course for the control room.

As he walked, seemingly out of nowhere his thoughts reverted to his high school years and the quick comment made by his football coach. This comment, made during practice in his junior year, lingered in his memory.

Early in the season, the coach had assigned Darren to the second squad, which in and of itself would have been understandable since the first string had to practice against someone. What wasn't helpful, and in fact had haunted Darren, was the unnecessary side comment the young coach made to anyone within earshot. Upon assigning Darren to the second practice squad, the coach said of Darren, ". . . *not really first string caliber anyway.*"

The young coach seemed oblivious to whether or not Darren even heard the comment. He seemed more interested in bolstering his own ego, which at that point in his life included glib comments about others. Maybe he had since learned the powerful impact that type of comment could have on someone and might have learned to contain them.

In Darren's case the damage was done and the ominous words still lingered. Though Darren didn't realize it, they had continued to influence him. He was less confident and trusting, a little more reserved, a little less inclined to be assertive. In spite of this, and all the other hindrances and obstacles he had overcome, Darren gave himself a little credit for what he had accomplished. He had become good at what he was doing professionally. He was beginning to be noticed as he remained diligent, was paying his dues, and making his way through the ranks.

He was, after all, competing for the lead reporter slot at the station, and several of his segments were scheduled to run on the evening news. He wondered what his old coach would have to say if he could see him now. More importantly, and largely responsible for the rise in Darren's self-esteem, was Paula. She was the woman who would hopefully wear the ring in Darren's pocket. She was also anchoring the evening news for the first time tonight. Often this late in the day, Darren would still be somewhere in the field. Something about today was very different. He sensed it was much more important for him to be here for her big day, than not to be.

Throwing his coat on the back of a chair behind camera three, he grabbed another chair, wheeled it up a little, and sat down quietly to watch the crew set up for the evening broadcast.

He glanced around the room at the banks of monitors. Several different feeds were streaming in. On one he saw something about the Middle East peace talks being held in Rome. Another was airing a montage of scenes from the many battlefronts throughout the Middle East and the Far East. It had gotten too dangerous to actually try to hold any kind of peace talks in the Middle East. For the past four months Rome had become the place where the civilized world hoped a miracle would happen. A seeming endless display of ambulances, smoke and fire, bloodied men, women and children, tears, anger, and despair dominated the monitors. Though many used the term "holy war," the conflict had become a very "unholy war".

Darren wasn't particularly religious. He'd leave that up to Paula, since she was more into God. Darren felt an unrelenting hopelessness as he looked at the seemingly unending scenes of terrorist attacks. "They're never going to get that Humpty Dumpty back together again - - - way too many parts to the puzzle," he said under his breath as he gazed at the spectacle.

Darren had spent nearly six months as a reporter in the Middle East and was uncomfortably familiar with the generational animosity between the Israelis and the Arab nations. He had spent so much time interviewing those caught in the crossfire that he had even begun to understand, in a rough sort of way, the Arabic language of the Palestinian locals. He could think of no aspect of his time there as being enjoyable or peaceful.

There was an ever-present feeling that something bad would happen at any moment. Everyone sensed it and dealt with it, whether they wanted to or not. He was relieved to have put all that behind him, and he had no intention of ever going back. He had made that clear to his superiors after he fulfilled his commitment and boarded the first available flight to get him out of what he considered a God-forsaken part of planet Earth.

Paula entered and quickly sat behind the news desk. Her poise and determined manner projected a confidence that well-obscured the insecurities and challenges of her adolescence. She was once preoccupied with a feeling that her ears were somehow unattractive and refused to style her hair in any manner that would reveal any more than the lower portion of her earlobes. That all

15

changed when Paula began to realize her real identity was in who God perceived her to be. She was no longer controlled by what others might think of her. As an outward declaration, she was again wearing her almond brown hair tied back with her very normal and modestly adorned ears in full display. Her green eyes had a slightly mesmerizing effect when she looked at you. At least that was the effect they had on Darren.

Darren sensed the activity and redirected his attention from the war footage to his future bride, or so he hoped. Sure, she was good-looking, nice and everything, but there was something else about her. It was difficult to put into words. It was as if there was some kind of invisible energy or warmth emulating from her. Darren wondered if anyone else sensed it. He figured it was probably just an indication of his love for her. He couldn't remember feeling that sensation before.

Though they were not childhood sweethearts who had known one another for years, it seemed to Darren like they had always been close and he could not imagine a future without her. When around her, the cares and concerns in his life lessened a little, and he felt more excited about life. It was weird, and he couldn't explain it, but he liked it. "Please say yes, please say yes," he whispered to himself as he watched the evening news. His eyes were fixed on Paula, the most exciting person on planet Earth.

The News 8 "On-the-Scene" team was set up to do a live remote from a newly renovated area of downtown Houston. James O'Brien was KNOW's man on the street. As the 5 o'clock news team seized the airwaves, James and his crew were getting ready to do a live interview with downtown resident Gladys White.

Paula began, "Welcome to the evening news. I'm Paula Roberts, along with Meredith Cameron with the weather and Justin Kline on sports." Paula opened with the big news of the day. "Once again, a terrorist explosion in Israel set a new one-day record for civilian casualties. Though the final numbers are not in..." Associate feeds of footage taken at the scene earlier in the day were beamed into the homes of approximately 11 percent of the Houston metropolitan area, KNOW's market share. The Channel 8 news machine was running smoothly. Paula displayed the poise and calm of a seasoned professional, even though it was her first time in the anchor chair.

Israel

On the other side of the world, in a blown-out abandoned warehouse in the terrorist-controlled part of Gaza, suicide bombers were putting the final touches on what was designed to be another in a long series of deadly attacks against Israel. Two recently commandeered police vehicles loaded with explosives slipped into the relatively quiet night. Their target was a Jewish wedding being held within a supposedly safe and secure zone well inside Israeli territory. The wedding ceremony was over, and the guests at the reception were relaxed, thanks to several hours of wine, dancing, and joyous celebration. The security also was a little relaxed after what had been a relatively quiet evening.

The terrorist leader, Fahad Mohammed, talked via cell phone to two young Arab drivers. He praised them in advance for their courageous act against Allah's great enemy, Israel. He remained on the line with them as they made their way toward their target. Fahad moved to the rooftop of his building to have an unobstructed view of the Jerusalem skyline and the carnage that was about to begin.

Houston

Paula did the intro setup for the live downtown remote. "And now we go live to James O'Brien, Houston's favorite man on the street. He is talking to some people who are not happy with the downtown renovation project." On screen was O'Brien, microphone in hand, with Gladys White standing to his left. As James began speaking, Gladys suddenly shifted her focus from the camera to the sky. As James turned to move the microphone toward her, his voice trailed off as he was just as suddenly distracted by something in the sky. By-standers in the crowd behind James and Gladys also began looking up. Finally, the camera operator panned the sky to show the viewing audience what was drawing all this attention.

The early evening sky was ablaze with a swirling and pulsating display of what looked somewhat like the northern lights, but generating unusually intense shapes, colors and patterns. Something like this might not have been a totally shocking event in the Polar Regions, but to the viewing audience of Channel 8, it was mesmerizing.

Israel

As Fahad, cell phone in hand, leaned against a pole, something beyond comprehension grabbed his total attention. The night sky over Jerusalem was ablaze in a frenzy of color, light, and motion. Stunned, he stumbled a few steps forward. The hand that held the cell phone drifted away from his ear. What he saw was the most dazzling display of lights and motion he had ever seen. He was spellbound. What did it mean?

Houston

The crowd, as well as the entire Channel 8 "On the Scene" crew, fixed their attention on the skies as they watched the dazzling overhead display. Much of the viewing audience of Channel 8 continued to watch the display on television, while others joined the many thousands who had gone outside to watch the spectacle.

A member of the station crew passed a message to Paula via headset, and she pressed her earpiece closer with her fingers. As he spoke to her, she reported the new information to her viewing audience. "It seems that the disturbance we have been watching is visible in other locations across the country, with some reports from as far away as New York. In fact - - - reports from all over the world are starting to come in. This visual phenomenon is global. For continued coverage on the atmospheric event, we now go live to GBS News in New York with this breaking story."

The control desk switched the feed from the local news desk to the national news feed. Paula and her colleagues sat motionless, not knowing what to do next. Darren approached the news desk, walking slowly toward Paula. Then, at about the time Darren reached the desk, the same thought occurred to both of them. Out loud and in unison, they each said "Stan."

Another wordless second or two, and then Paula reached for her purse as Darren grabbed his coat. They hurried from the newsroom and headed for the parking garage and Darren's four-wheel-drive SUV.

Channel 8 personnel streamed out of the building to see the light show. Paula and Darren made a quick stop and got approval from the station manager on their plan. Cleared for the mission, they would not be missed for some time.

They headed for NASA's Johnson Space Center thirty miles southeast of Houston. Stan, a good friend for many years, was the center's director of systems engineering. If anyone knew anything about what was going on in the heavens, it would be Stan.

Israel

Fahad was dazed and confused by what he was seeing. What did it mean? Was this some new Israeli defense device? Was it some Israeli warning system? Were they onto his plan? Was Allah trying to tell him to hold off? He wondered whether setting off explosions in the middle of Allah's display of his great power over the Holy City would be insulting. He followed this line of thought, raised the cell phone to his ear, and called off the attack. He directed the two suicide drivers back to the warehouse. For the moment, the late-night wedding guests were spared as they too looked skyward.

Fahad paused and searched for the words to use for his next call. Though he felt he had done the right thing, trying to explain it to his superior, who was also his older brother Ahmed, made him somewhat fearful. Ahmed, already in route to the United States on his own mission, had little tolerance for failure or deviations from his plans. Apprehensive or not, Fahad had to make the call. He entered the numbers that would connect him to the other, and for now more peaceful, side of the world.

Chapter 2

Twilight's Last Gleaming

The celestial light show did not go unnoticed in Rome, either. As usual, the peace talks were stalled, and nerves were well past the limit of human resolve. Although still seriously divided, the individual factions of the Arab world were working together, born of their common hatred of Israel and the United States.

The appropriate political emissaries from all the key players in the region, and many from several of the not-so-significant ones, were at the negotiations. Even here, participants seized the opportunity to recess and observe what was apparently a world-wide atmospheric event. For a brief moment, normal life on Earth was put on hold as everyone stopped to look toward the sky. Drug dealers, thieves, politicians, mothers, soldiers, preachers, business people, teachers, and terrorists set aside everything that usually drove and controlled them. For a brief time there was an unexpected moment of peace on earth, as all humanity paused to ponder the heavens.

Darren and Paula sped down Interstate 45 in Darren's white SUV toward the NASA complex. Paula was on her cell phone with Meredith Cameron back at the station, telling her of their plans. Meredith agreed to cover for them and confirmed that New York would be handling things until further notice. Worldwide news outlets were inundated with reports on the atmospheric phenomenon.

The traffic on the interstate was a little lighter than normal, with cars parked on the shoulders as their occupants stood outside and watched the light show. The two reporters could hardly contain their excitement and their anticipation over the inside track they felt they had with Stan. They were eager to find out what was going on.

Darren nervously shouted at some motorists who looked as if they were preparing to merge back onto the freeway. "Just stay there! Whoa!"

Darren was driving faster than he should have and Paula, who normally wouldn't have put up with Darren's speeding, instead urged him on. "Go! Go! Look out! OK...OK...just go!"

Darren wheeled the SUV through the main gates at the complex, and he and Paula flashed their IDs to the guard at the security gate checkpoint. "We're here to meet with Stan Woodman. We just talked to him on the phone, and he said he'd call you to authorize our entry," said Darren.

The soldier looked back to the guard station and skeptically asked the sergeant in the guardhouse, "Channel 8 news?" The sergeant waved them through. The SUV powered through the gate. When they had just barely cleared the gate, the NASA lockdown alarm sounded as the heavy-duty security gate slid across the main entrance, completely barring access to the space center.

Stan was holding the parking garage access door open as the SUV pulled up. Stan briefly smiled as they pulled to a stop close to the elevator. With his hand he beckoned them to hurry as they got out of the vehicle.

"Hey guys," said Stan. "Let's go, let's go. There's a lot going on, and I'm late for a meeting they just called. Go to my office and wait. You know the way. The door is open." Stan stepped into the main building and pointed to a waiting elevator.

Stan warned them, "Don't go snooping around. The whole place is buzzing, and you look a little out of place, OK?" As the door closed behind him, the Channel 8 reporters entered the waiting elevator, as Stan hurried down the hallway. Immediately after entering, Paula jumped back out, causing the automatic doors to abruptly stop closing and slide open.

"What...what's up?" Darren asked.

"Bathroom," replied Paula. "The bathroom on this floor is decent. The one on the fifth floor...well, this one's definitely nicer, and I can't wait. It'll only take a minute."

Darren agreed. "Yeah, OK. Yeah, I'm going too." They left their assigned elevator, entered the corridor of the main administrative building and headed for the restrooms located a short distance down the hallway. A few minutes later they exited the restrooms at nearly the same time, paused for a moment, and tried to collect their thoughts as they focused on one another.

"My heart's pounding so hard - - - I feel like I did before a football game in high school!" said Darren.

"Mine too," agreed Paula. "It's not every day that the sky lights up, especially right in the middle of a broadcast!"

One last clothes straightening and they turned to head for the elevator. They both froze as the sound of multiple conversations and footsteps signaled the approach of a sizeable crowd.

Rushing down the corridor, Paula tried the first available door in hopes of finding a place where they could hide. It was open. They hustled into the room, identified only as 'auditorium', and sought further refuge inside a small sound booth in the upper section of the room. The auditorium was designed to easily hold several hundred people.

With the sounds growing louder, they cowered together and waited for the crowd to pass. Suddenly, the doors of the auditorium room swung open, and the noisy crowd filed in. Wide-eyed and staring at one another, Paula and Darren remained motionless and tried to remain invisible in the shadows of the unused sound booth.

The group, around 40 strong, walked past the sound room down toward the stage and filled in the seats closest to the front of the auditorium. To the partial relief of the two reporters, the group was located some distance from the sound room. Someone's voice rose slightly, and the chatter began to subside.

"Must be the guy in charge." whispered Darren.

Mr. Man-in-Charge continued. "OK, OK. Let's go over where we are and make sure we're all on the same page. First, are we sure it's still there? It didn't get burned up or something like that?"

Another voice. "Still there, sir, and it is in what has been verified as a sustainable orbit - - - a little shaky, but it should sustain."

Even though they were several yards from the group and were straining to hear, the trespassers caught almost every word. They opened the sound room door slightly so they could hear better.

Mr. Man-in-Charge again. "We the only ones who know?"

A female voice. "We think so. It was a fluke that we even caught it. The shuttle crew was in the middle of a military satellite upgrade when one of the crew members happened to see the sun reflecting off it as it passed within a mile of the shuttle. The crew reported it to ground, and we were able to lock onto it. If they knew where to look, the Russians, the Chinese, and probably the Japanese could see it. They have the capability.

"The good thing is that it's very small, and with its nonconventional orbit, there's a good chance nobody will notice it for weeks. With all the visual activity in the upper atmosphere, there will be a great deal of focus on the sky. So, let's just say we were at the right place at the right time. All we can count on is that we've got the jump on the rest of the world. Since the decommissioning of the shuttle program, we as the military have control of the remaining shuttle fleet. And we currently do have one shuttle and crew already in orbit."

The Man-in-Charge asked, "And we're sure this is the real thing, not just space debris or a piece of something we sent up there and lost track of?"

A new voice. "General, the odds of something coming into a sustainable orbit, something with a highly polished cylindrical shape and at just the right speed, and it not being intelligently designed is, well, just about incalculable. There's some kind of craft or machine up there, and it didn't come from anywhere on our planet."

So the Man-in-Charge was also a general. Interesting, Paula thought. Darren's expression indicated he was thinking the same thing.

The general questioned further. "Is it retrievable? Would it fit in the space shuttle?"

The female voice again. "Well, not without some major cargo reshuffling, but our people think it might be possible. Initially it will be a little tricky considering its erratic tumbling, but so far they think it can be done. Based on its relatively small size, we think it's a probe and not a life-supporting vehicle."

"Has the shuttle changed course?" the general asked.

This time it was Stan who answered. "Yes, sir. In anticipation of a retrieval order, they are already initiating course-matching burns and should be in position in thirty-six hours - - - that is, if it's a go."

"And the lights, all that atmospheric light show—coincidence? Part of this deal? Germs, viruses? Some kind of weapon?" the general continued.

A second female voice, a little tentative at first, responded. "Not very likely sir. The best guess, and the group's pretty much together on this, is that wherever this thing came from, it picked up a trail of cosmic dust. There's no telling how long it's been traveling, maybe centuries. A lot of debris was picked up over time and got dragged along with it. Now why it's dragging so much more cosmic debris than its size would warrant is anybody's guess. When it came into orbit Earth's magnetic field grabbed the dust, and the result is the light show."

"How long should this light effect last?" the general asked.

Female number two responded, "Less than a week, give or take a few days, and gradually subsiding day by day."

Paula and Darren heard footsteps. Someone from the group in search of an ashtray for his cigar was approaching the sound room. The sound of the footsteps grew louder. Suddenly, the door to the booth swung open. Startled, Paula and Darren were face-to-face with an equally startled General Foster C. Adams, the Man-in-Charge.

Chapter 3

Agreements and Findings

The general immediately summoned security to escort the media intruders and detain them in a conference room down the hall. As they sat at the conference table for a seemingly interminable amount of time, the two reporters began to feel the weight of the predicament they were in. With armed soldiers stationed both in the room and outside the door, their conversation was not exactly free flowing.

Darren, a little strained and with a slight hint of *"it's your fault, you know,"* asked Paula, "So, is the restroom on the fifth floor really all that terrible?" Before Paula could answer, the doors burst open and the general, Stan, and several others entered the room. There was no chatter. The group sat quickly and prepared for what was to come. Technicians set up audio recording devices and also a video camcorder.

When everyone was ready, Stan began. "I've explained to the general who you are, that you are here on my invitation, and that you're not here illegally, or with malice, or with the intention of creating a breach in national security."

Then the general took over. "It is unfortunate for us, as well as for the both of you, that this happened, but there's nothing we can do about it right now. We all have to play the game from where we're at. Maybe you only heard a little, maybe a lot, but it doesn't matter. Fact is, we can't risk this getting out, especially right now and to the media. We're not even sure what were dealing with, and we don't need any more complications or scrutiny till we do.

"So here's the deal. We will give you an inside track on this operation with the explicit understanding and agreement that absolutely no information will be released without our authorization. We have prepared several documents for you to sign. Should you fail to honor our agreement, there will be a painful, long, and uncomfortable detainment for both of you. I don't care if we need to use national security, the war powers act, homeland security, the IRS, or whatever. Just know that if you blow this deal, you're going to spend the better part of the rest of your lives smothered in a mountain of red tape and a legal quagmire that will haunt you, your children, and your children's children!"

There was a pregnant pause as General Adams waited for his words to register. Eyeball to eyeball, he alternately stared at each of them. The general didn't blink. The contrite couple did and then looked at each other.

"An inside track doesn't sound too bad," Darren said.

"Yeah, I think I could live with that," Paula agreed.

"Yeah, OK, I think we could do that," Darren added, a bit too casually.

The general cut in with a sobering response. "This is no joke! You screw this up, and trust me - - - you will pay a price you do not want to pay!" He waited.

Darren and Paula quickly nodded. They got the message. "Yes, you have our complete attention and understanding, sir" Paula said.

"We won't mess this up, sir," Darren assured General Adams.

"If you do, you can all but forget your journalism career. Am I making myself clear?"

"Waterford clear, sir," Darren replied.

The general looked puzzlingly at Stan since he wasn't sure what Darren meant. Stan offered assistance. "I think what Darren means is not only are things 'crystal clear', they are 'Waterford crystal clear" - - - "It's his way of saying they are *extremely clear* - - - some of that new style street talk I guess."

Darren concurred. "Yes, sir, that's what it means, sorry sir."

"It's a deal then?" The general asked sternly.

"It's a deal," the two replied in unison.

They then willingly signed the documents.

Then Stan, who seemed to Darren to be a bit keyed up, led them to his office. Darren wasn't sure if Stan's behavior was due to the trouble they had caused or the stress related to the atmospheric phenomenon.

General Adams had dangled a tempting carrot before them. They would have access to inside information about the attempt to retrieve the object however, at the moment they had a muzzle the size of Texas firmly in place.

"Uh, Stan, are we going to have access to real information, or did the general just tell us that but really plan to throw a few scraps now and then for show?" Darren asked.

Stan stayed true to the task at hand, which appeared to be organizing his desk. He answered as he worked. "No, you're going to get the real stuff, at least that's my understanding. The general can be a real pain, but he says what he means and means what he says. If he said it, he'll do it. That is, unless he gets redirected from above, which does sometimes happen."

"Has anything like this happened before? Area 51 kind of activity?" asked Paula. Stan smiled and flopped into his chair.

"Not really. I mean, we do have a facility out there, but it's not what the tabloids say. It's really more of a solar propulsion research operation. So there's no aliens or alien docking stations with visitors from other worlds checking in or checking out."

"How are we supposed to get the information?" asked Paula.

"The general and I talked about that. I guess part of my penance for getting you two involved is that you go through me," answered Stan.

"So how much are you at liberty to tell us?" asked Darren.

Stan leaned forward and addressed Paula. "Darren and I go way back, some ten years before you and I met. Look guys, I feel closer to both of you than anybody else around here. What I know you will know, unless it's something that would get you into more trouble than you are already in. From where I'm sitting, I can't even imagine more trouble than this."

With that, Paula brought the meeting to a close. "Now *that's* what I call a real deal."

Albuquerque, New Mexico

Pastor Russell Brooks or "Pastor Russ", as the congregation liked to call him, stepped to the pulpit of Albuquerque's Freedom Church. The church had experienced considerable growth recently, and Pastor Russ was in the process of trying to keep all the new faces and names straight. It was the Wednesday mid-week service, and the church was nearly full. The much larger-than-normal-crowd was no doubt due to the "SkyFire" phenomenon. This was the media's hot new name for the light show that started the night before.

Most media sources were devoting significant time to asking a number of well-known religious personalities if the SkyFire event was a prophetic sign signaling the imminent return of Jesus. Many of the guests came across as flaky, while those who appeared more credible suggested that although the event could be tied to biblical end-times prophecy; it could also just be an unusual atmospheric phenomenon. Time would reveal the truth.

Pastor Russ addressed the anxious crowd. "I know that the recent light display in the sky has been a source of entertainment for many and also a cause of concern for many others who are fearful that it may be a sign that the end is near. What I want to speak to you about tonight is faith. I don't know the cause of this light in the sky or how long it will last, but I am confident that the God we serve was not surprised by the event. He knew thousands of years ago that we would all be staring at the sky above and wondering what it all meant.

"Nevertheless, whatever the cause, God is not shaken, and neither should we be. Whether lights in the sky, storms on a rolling sea, a desperate financial situation, or a grim report from the doctor, we are to keep our eyes fixed on Him, the author and finisher of our faith."

The pastor began slowly moving in front of the congregation as he continued his message. "I want to share a story with you tonight that some of you may have already heard. Years ago in a liberal college, a Christian student found himself in a large chemistry lecture class. As the story goes, his instructor was an avowed atheist and was aware of the student's belief in Christ. One day the instructor challenged the student to an experiment that would prove whether or not God existed. The student, put on the spot in front of the class, listened to the proposed terms of the experiment.

"The instructor held up a light bulb and proposed to drop the bulb on the bare concrete floor, which he contended would shatter the bulb. Now, this was no high-tech, shatter-resistant bulb. Back then, you dropped a light bulb, and you cleaned up light bulb pieces.

"The professor smugly suggested that the student pray to his God to keep the light bulb from breaking. Whether the bulb broke or not was supposed to prove or disprove the existence of God.

"The student took his time as he considered all the implications of agreeing to the challenge. The student was willing, but requested one concession. He asked that the so-called experiment be conducted in three days, on the following Friday. He explained that this would give the student and his friends time to fast and pray about it. The student's request triggered repressed laughter from the non-believing students in the class. The instructor, thrilled at the prospect of crushing the belief of the small contingent of believers on campus, quickly agreed.

"Well, Friday came, and the lecture hall was filled to overflowing as news of the 'great experiment' made its way throughout the campus. Even some local news reporters were on hand to cover the event. The instructor was eager to show these Christians the folly of their faith.

"When the time came, anticipation was thick in the air. The instructor walked to the podium. He removed the light bulb from a paper bag and held it out at arm's length. Not wanting to take the slightest chance, he raised his arm to elevate the bulb nearly another foot higher, to about seven feet off the concrete floor.

"For several seconds he stood motionless. It became very quiet, and every eye in the room was fixed on that light bulb. The professor quickly released his grip, and left the bulb to the mercy of gravity and the cold, hard, concrete floor below.

"As he released his grip, something strange happened. It seemed something sticky must have gotten on the instructor's thumb. Instead of falling straight down, the light bulb was pulled by the sticky thumb toward the instructor as it fell. The light bulb hit the instructor's leg just above the knee and slid down the lower part of his leg and right across the top of the instructor's shoe.

"Deflected by his shoe and traveling horizontally, the bulb slid across the concrete floor and came to a stop right in front of the student—unbroken! Several seconds of silence followed as everyone tried to digest what they had just seen. Then the lecture hall erupted. The Christians were jumping and cheering, and the nonbelievers were crying foul."

Pastor Russ began walking back toward the pulpit and continued. "And so the great college experiment to prove the existence of God, well, for many, proved nothing at all. For the believers and those willing to believe, the unseen hand of God was evident. For those who were determined to resist the things of God, well He made a way for them to continue in their unbelief. To them, it was just coincidence, a fluke; it didn't prove anything."

The pastor was now back at the pulpit and brought his message to a close. "Where faith is, so also is the mysterious hand of God. Jesus' nail-scarred hands reach across time and space, and beckon us even today. Some of the most important words God ever spoke came when Jesus challenged not only His disciples, but all humanity to make the decision to *'have faith in God'*. When calamity or catastrophe, disease, despair, victory, or defeat, or even when wildfire light dances across the open sky and confronts us, God dares us to focus on, and put our faith in, Him. He will not fall short or fail those who make the decision to *have faith in Him*."

Washington, DC

Two starkly different sets of findings were included in the next morning's presidential

45

briefing. One was a secret status report on NASA's ongoing SkyFire retrieval attempt. The president was keenly interested in the effort to secure the object before its existence became known. Though his schedule was well-established for weeks in advance, his people were busy looking for a way to accommodate an onsite visit to view the object firsthand, provided the retrieval attempt proved successful. The object was to be secured at the military facility at White Sands, New Mexico.

The scramble was on to bring the president near the site without drawing unwanted attention and without visibly deviating from his disclosed travel commitments. His staff settled on the annual Albuquerque International Balloon Festival. This festival would give the president an excuse to be in the region and an opportunity to make a clandestine, off-route visit to the White Sands Missile Range.

Coordination of the presidential travel protocols began to make their way through the appropriate "secure" channels. The prospective plan for the president to observe the object would be in place before the object was even retrieved by the shuttle. Not only did this "Balloon Festival" development set the presidential travel team in action, it also fit well with a plan devised on the other side of the globe. If successful, this foreign-designed plan would destroy any prospect for world peace for some time to come.

Among the many reports and findings on the president's desk was one that would have looked more sinister had not so many similar reports preceded it. Within it, yet without specific details, some of the reports monitoring terrorist "chatter" indicated that something substantial was approaching and possibly imminent. The most unnerving aspect was a period of intensifying chatter and then a subsequent and troubling silence.

Following the silence and the corresponding escalation of terrorist activities, the recent horrific bombings suggested that an intensified level of terrorist activities might be beginning. As a precaution, the threat level was raised to high. Unless and until further specific information became available, no further direct action was to be taken.

48

Chapter 4

Rain Dance

Many cultures throughout the world have a similar version of a universal story. Native American medicine men, biblical prophets, and spiritual leaders from all regions of the planet have their own "getting ready for rain" story. It's a story about preparing for the hoped-for, prayed-for, and sometimes danced-for event.

As Native Americans performed a rain dance, tribal elders taught the youth how to bring faith and expectation together. Not only did they teach the ritual of the dance itself, but they also showed their young how to build catch basins for even a small amount of rain. It was a demonstration of their faith and belief that the desired event would actually happen.

In a similar fashion, the SkyFire event initiated a flurry of preparation on a grand scale. From the president down to the engineer working on the slightest detail of the project, everyone involved was impacted by this small object circling planet Earth. Every human and material resource that NASA needed, NASA got, regardless of cost. An event like this defined the agency and its space program. This was the big enchilada, and NASA in its own way, was preparing for rain.

Agency officials got to work on a cover-up story. Press releases spun the story that SkyFire resulted from an unexpected encounter with debris trailing a small magnetically charged asteroid. All the news outlets were telling the same story, each quoting its own official and properly credentialed atmospheric expert.

Helping to quell the SkyFire fervor that had dominated the airwaves was news of an apparent breakthrough in the Middle East peace talks. The newly elected Israeli prime minister, along with the leaders of the surrounding Arab countries, made a joint announcement from the peace conference in Rome. All the key players, including the Hamas-controlled Palestinian state, were present to validate the elaborate agreement.

Never before had any agreement been able to garner the support of all the factions involved. Drafted in large part by the Israeli prime minister and the emerging charismatic leader of Hamas, the accord seemed to offer something for everyone.

As the intensity of the light show began fading and the spotlight of the world refocused on peace in the Middle East, the space shuttle closed in on a cylinder slowly tumbling through space. Extreme precautions were taken to obscure the clandestine mission in progress. Since the shuttle was on a military satellite maintenance mission, military protocols were already in effect.

Darren and Paula were the only non-governmental personnel in the loop, and they were given a workstation in NASA's mission control ready room where they could observe the retrieval attempt. After some governmental string pulling, Channel 8 relieved them of their usual responsibilities so they could focus on SkyFire and provide periodic updates. They were given a substantial degree of leeway from regular station policies and reporting.

The two watched as four spacewalking astronauts used their handheld propulsion thruster packs to reach the object. Though it was difficult, they were able to attach several magnetic portable thrusters to the slowly tumbling cylinder. By using remote radio control transmitters, they were able to trigger the portable thrusters to slow down and then stop the erratic tumbling.

Twenty minutes after the orbit synchronization effort began, the shuttle and the cylindrical object moved in unison and were slowly brought closer together. Measurements verified that the cylinder would fit into the cargo bin, but stowing it meant removing the shuttle's cargo.

The original cargo, a group of replacement component modules for military satellites, was unloaded by the shuttle's robotic arm and tethered together for later retrieval. Then came the first hint of something that NASA had not anticipated. It was something that would dominate every aspect of the retrieval attempt. It came in the form of a communication from the shuttle commander.

The amount of thruster fuel used to steady the object was far beyond the amount they had expected to use. Their portable thruster supply was all but exhausted. Nevertheless, the object was steadied and prepared for retrieval.

The shuttle's robotic arm moved to the cylinder and grasped the object. As soon as the arm operator started to move the object, overload sensors on the arm began to trigger. There was no imminent danger of significant damage to the arm, but whatever the object was by Earth's standards, it was heavy.

Working in the freedom of their weightless environment, the crew was able to move the cylinder into the cargo hold with relative ease. The warning bells and alarm flashes of the robotic arms overload sensors tripped every time the mechanics of the robotic system were engaged to move or stop the cylinder.

Once inside the shuttle, the cylinder was secured to the static motion-sensor plate used to get accurate weight measurements of objects in the weightlessness of space. The plate was moved slowly forward and backward while resistance sensors determined the actual sea-level weight of the object.

At first it seemed the system must be broken. Based on the size, dimensions, and probable mix of mass and dead space of a device that size, NASA engineers would have likely estimated its weight at around 10,000 pounds. It was registering an unfathomable 77,000 pounds! As the weight reading was announced on NASA's secure communications link, everyone, except the mission's media guests, was keenly aware of the significance of this huge complication. Landing the space shuttle with that kind of weight on board was well beyond the shuttle's structural capability.

Sensing the wave of concern, Paula questioned the aide assigned to them. "Is there a problem?"

"I'm not exactly sure what the critical load-factor capability is on the shuttle, but if the weight reading we just heard is correct, I don't think re-entry is possible," Lieutenant Stevens answered and continued. "The shuttle is not made to push back through the atmosphere with that kind of weight on board. Not enough slow-down capability, not enough wing for the weight on board - - - she'll come in too fast, especially when she gets to the denser atmosphere closer to the surface. I'm not an expert, but I'm afraid it might not be possible."

Without a word, the two journalists rose and headed for Stan's office. Stan wasn't there, so they waited.

As time dragged on, fidgeting gave way to sleeping in their chairs. It was almost an hour before Stan returned to his office and quietly began making coffee. The aroma awakened Paula first. She'd always had a thing for coffee, ever since she first drank it with her father when she was ten. She started out using cream and sugar, but by the time she was eleven she was taking it black. She placed her hands around the generous ceramic cup Stan had placed in front of her. She savored the aroma and extracted the warmth from the handmade cup, identified only by the word *"Improvise."* By then, Darren was beginning to stir.

Stan began the update. "Well, do you know what's going on? About the slight little problem we encountered?"

"You mean about the excessive weight of the thing?" Darren replied.

"Yeah, the 'thing,'" Stan responded, somewhat sarcastically.

Paula jumped in. "Can it be done? Is it possible?"

"At first I didn't think so," Stan said. "But the general gave the order to find a way, and that's what we've been working on."

"So is there a way?" asked Darren.

Stan ambled slowly around his desk and sat down. "It's crazy, but there's an outside chance it could work."

"We're all ears," said Darren.

Stan started describing the plan that some of the best brains on the planet were fine-tuning. "We start by stripping the shuttle cargo and even nonessential parts of the shuttle itself. We had already planned to attempt landing at White Sands in New Mexico, just north of El Paso. It's remote enough so we can secure it, yet it has one of the longest alternate runways available.

"We're going to initiate what we call a high-inclination re-entry, implement reverse trajectory positioning, which is all actually pretty standard; but we'll be working it to the max. We plan to use all the available fuel, except for the minimal amount needed for critical emergency maneuvering. This will slow the orbital velocity much more than usual. The gain achieved in orbital speed reduction will be offset to a certain extent by the corresponding greater influence of gravity.

"We've worked the numbers every way possible and this seems to be the best approach given all the factors. Makes it a little trickier bringing her in, but we've got to work with what we've got, not with what we wish we had."

Stan paused slightly and then resumed. "In order to try to dodge the re-entry heat bullet, some wild things are in store. Since the shuttle crew is at risk, everyone but the three-man crew necessary to bring it down needs to be dropped off at the space station. The three-man—or should I say, two-man, one-woman re-entry crew knows the odds aren't in their favor. They all volunteered without hesitation because they figured it's worth it.

"At the appropriate point in the burn they're going to flip it back around before they get too superheated and continue a somewhat normal re-entry. They are taking into consideration the jet stream and are trying to avoid it to achieve the best deceleration possible. They're going to deploy the main drag chute early, knowing full well that they won't make it all the way. Then they'll use the first backup chute system until it goes, and then they'll use the second backup system until it fails or hopefully holds. Every other factor available is likewise being taken into consideration. They're even figuring in the moon's gravitational effect, as well as the sun's.

"Lastly, they're building several huge portable catch nets similar to what they use on aircraft carriers. There will be six sets in all, each one consisting of two eighteen-wheel tractor-trailers with the catch-net stretched between them. They're mobile, and the plan is to have them stationed at intermittent ready points along the runway. The nets themselves are made of micro-Kevlar-filament line that are lightweight, extremely strong and move through the air with a minimal amount of wind resistance. They'll closely monitor the shuttle's descent and attempt to time their speed to match the intercept point with the shuttle approximate to touchdown.

"The modified eighteen-wheel tractor-trailers will be running close to a hundred miles an hour for the attempt. Since the shuttle should be traveling well over normal touchdown speeds and tire capability specifications, it's going to be quite a jolt when the nets, hopefully, catch the shuttle and the drag chutes on the nets themselves actually open. We need all the pieces of the plan to do their part to have a chance."

Stan continued. "All the simulations we've run so far don't result in a successful landing, but then again we're operating outside the working ranges of heat panels, tires, drag chutes, craft structural integrity, and so on. And the simulations utilize the capacities and work ranges with only a certain degree of tolerance and leeway. There's no data at all on using catch nets on something like the space shuttle."

"So," Paula asked, "do you think it will work?"

"Realistically, probably not. Just too many factors stretched a little too far. If I were a betting man, I'd say we'll be lucky to be picking up sizeable pieces. The jet stream and the catch nets are the big wild cards. If we get a break with the stream, and if we pass through just right, and if we're lucky enough to actually catch it with some of the nets, maybe, just maybe, we'll have a shot."

Chapter 5

Road Trip

By the end of day two, Darren and Paula were free of their regular responsibilities at the station. After a frantic roundup of the essentials needed for the trip to White Sands, Darren picked up Paula at her apartment.

"Got the cooler?" asked Paula as she closed the door and secured her seatbelt.

"Yeah, sure do. But I couldn't find the smoothie drinks you like. The store didn't have them, or at least I couldn't find them."

"I guess when you really want to get something done, you need to send a woman in," Paula teased. The condescending look from Darren let Paula know that she hit her mark. The couple had gotten into a no-real-harm-intended competition in the male vs. female thing. Given the intensity of current events, they both looked forward to this sudden working vacation that just dropped out of the sky.

Darren donned his Terminator-style shades and steered the SUV onto the access ramp of Interstate 10 heading west toward New Mexico.

As they escaped the Houston metro area and traffic started to thin, Darren relaxed a little and started talking to Paula. When he didn't hear her respond, he looked over only to find that she was fast asleep. They were both tired from all the commotion and excitement, and Darren was actually relieved to see her getting some rest. Maybe she could catch up on her sleep, and if he could stay awake for another five or six hours, they could switch and he could catch up on his sleep. He popped three pieces of gum in his mouth, which was his stay-awake strategy, and turned the radio on. The music was just loud enough to keep his mind engaged but not loud enough to disturb his intended future bride.

In the wee hours of the morning, Darren figured they were about a hundred miles from El Paso. He was tired and pulled off the interstate and into a truck stop somewhere around Van Horn, Texas. The jostling of the vehicle over ruts made by the heavy truck traffic caused Paula to stir. Darren planned on fueling the vehicle and hoped she was ready to drive. If not, he was going to do some coffee and walk around a bit.

Like the Energizer bunny, Paula popped up, did the hair and makeup thing, and was out of the car and heading inside before Darren got his seat belt unhooked. By the time Darren was done fueling and had used the restroom, Paula was back in the vehicle, sitting behind the wheel and adjusting the rearview mirror.

"You're good to go?" Darren asked as he slid onto the passenger seat, still slightly warm from Paula's presence.

"I'm good," Paula responded as she pulled back onto the interstate. Wound up and ready to talk, Paula began firing away. "You know, this could be a big deal. I mean, if this ends up being an alien encounter, the whole world is going to freak." She looked over to make sure Darren was listening, only to find that he was already out. Looking at the time, 4:37 a.m., she refocused her attention on the road ahead. She had gotten more than seven hours of decent sleep. Touching his arm, Paula said, "You did well, D, you did really well."

Around ninety miles down the road, traffic began to slow down and eventually came to a stop. Paula could see the string of red tail lights trailing off ahead into the distance. Every few seconds the line would move ahead, only to stop again. This process kept repeating, and Paula figured she was probably averaging about a mile an hour. At this rate their arrival would be delayed by hours, and they would miss the landing. She assumed there had been a bad accident. Little by little she made her way toward the flashing lights ahead. By now, Darren was half-awake because of all the starting and stopping. When she finally got close enough, she could see no trace of an accident.

The delay turned out to be caused by an INS checkpoint, one of many that were starting to appear close to the Texas-Mexico border. INS agents were stopping each car and asking the same questions as they scrutinized the interior of the vehicles with their flashlights. Soon, it was Paula's turn.

"Are you a U. S. citizen?" asked the agent standing outside her door.

"Yes, we are," replied Paula.

Without hesitation and oblivious to Paula's answer for the both of them, the agent asked Darren directly, "And you, sir?"

"Yes, me too," responded a very tired-looking and red-eyed Darren.

"Can I see your driver's licenses, your identification papers?"

Paula dug in her purse, and Darren pulled his wallet out of his back pocket. Paula handed both IDs to the agent. While this was going on, other agents were peering through the heavily tinted rear windows of the SUV. They were trying to see if someone was hiding among the coolers, suitcases, and hanging clothes. The tinted windows didn't make it easy. The agent examined their IDs and then turned and spoke to one of the other guards. Paula was beginning to feel more and more uncomfortable.

The agent focused his attention on Paula and handed the IDs back. "OK. Ms. Roberts, I need you to pull ahead and off to the side for your vehicle to be checked." Darren started to groan but then quickly caught himself. Maybe there was something that triggered the agent's interest in their vehicle, or maybe it was a random selection.

In any event, this delay could easily prevent them from reaching White Sands in time.

Obeying the agent's instruction, Paula drove to the designated inspection area and waited. It appeared that they would be next to have their vehicle inspected, as soon as the agents finished with the minivan in front of them. As the family in the van watched, every object in the tightly packed van was removed and stacked on the pavement. Soon one of the agents turned his attention to the stacked cargo and began looking through each item. It was apparent they were looking for more than just illegal immigrants. They were probably looking for drugs or some other type of contraband.

As the process continued, Paula's annoyance began to escalate. They did not have time for this, and arriving late was becoming more and more a certainty.

After ten excruciatingly slow minutes, the agent in charge of the inspection team directed Paula to drive the vehicle to the inspection area. At about the same time that she put the SUV in park, another INS vehicle pulled right up to the inspection area, and a rather large and formidable looking INS agent got out of the vehicle. He walked right up to Paula's window and looked inside.

Satisfied with his observation, the new INS agent turned to the head of the inspection team. "I'll be taking these through. You and your team move on to the next vehicle."

The inspection team leader began to protest. As he did, the new agent just looked at his protesting colleague and never said a word. The protesting agent seemed to space out.

The inspection team leader broke his eye contact with the new agent and turned to his team. "OK, were going to move to the next vehicle. This one's OK. Let it through."

The interrupting agent then abruptly turned to Paula and said, "Follow me." With that, the agent returned to his vehicle, made a u-turn, and headed back in the direction from which he had come. Paula followed and soon they were free of the impasse. The agent ahead pulled over and waved them on with his oversized left arm.

"Thank You, Lord," said Paula as she brought the SUV back up to highway speed.

"And thank you, Mr. INS Agent, for getting us out of that mess," said Darren.

Paula quickly looked at Darren and responded, "So you really think that we just happened to get a friendly INS agent who came out of nowhere and escorted us through?"

Paula kept her attention on the road ahead as she paused to see if Darren had any response. Hearing none she sarcastically added. "Yeah, right, I guess we just got lucky."

***

Darren did not enjoy the same sound sleep that Paula had enjoyed. Around El Paso the traffic cut his siesta short, and by 7:30 a.m. he was sitting upright, a little frazzled-looking and about half awake. The military had reserved two separate rooms for them at a motel closest to the base side of town.

All Darren wanted to do was check in and flop on the closest available bed. Sometimes you don't get what you want, and it looked as if it was going to be one of those days. Darren started doing some mental figuring. Maybe there would be enough time to catch a power nap in the room. Even a half hour sounded wonderful to him. Their slow rush-hour progress was evaporating that hope.

"Now when did they figure the thing would be coming in again?" he asked Paula.

"Around 11 a.m. local time, if I remember right. If we don't take too long at the motel we just might make it."

"Man, I was really hoping to lie down for a while."

"Well, you can," Paula responded. "But you'll probably miss the whole thing."

After about five quiet minutes, Paula revisited her thoughts of the night before. "You know, while you were sleeping, I was thinking about all of this. I started talking to you last night, but you were already out." Darren turned his head toward Paula to appear that he was actually listening. It required effort, and he wasn't totally engaged. He was exhausted, but his sixth sense told him he at least better look as if he was paying attention.

Assuming he was on board, Paula continued. Her excitement over where they were and what they were about to witness animated her as she spoke. "This is a big deal! If this turns out to be an alien spaceship, well, it's huge. It'll be the biggest thing going on. There is a part of me that feels threatened a little, from a believer perspective. I know you think I'm a little too into this God thing, but if there is actual proof that aliens exist, well, this could shake up beliefs all over the world. I mean, its one thing to think about aliens and to read some of far out stuff in the tabloids, but to actually have proof. I...I...I just can't imagine it!"

Trying to sound coherent, Darren threw in a weak and not too convincing, "Yeah, me too."

Paula realized he was just going through the motions in an effort to be a supportive traveling companion. "Why don't you lie back again and catch a little more rest?" she offered, trying to let him off the "stay awake with me" hook. Too late. He was near asleep again now and oblivious to the traffic that surrounded the vehicle.

Chapter 6

One in the Hand

Time did not permit stopping by the motel. Tired but functioning, they were escorted to the observation area of the White Sands military base. Stan and several of the other players they had gotten to know back in Houston were already there. General Adams, noticing their arrival, made his way over for a conciliatory visit. If the story turned into something big, he wanted to be cast in a positive light by the media.

The general opened, "Glad to see you two made it. I was beginning to think someone forgot to keep you in the loop or that you got delayed somehow."

More small talk followed, but the large elevated countdown clock indicating the estimated time of touchdown was difficult to ignore: one hour and eleven minutes. It was almost as if the clock with its digital second-by-second countdown was infecting everyone with the enormity of the event.

The journalists were on the verge of exploding on the inside as all the excitement within kept building. How would they endure another whole hour? Using one another's presence to focus on, they calmed themselves. They sat at their assigned table, identified by a large fold-up place indicator. It was hard to sit still with their engines revved up. All traces of the fatigue Darren was experiencing earlier were gone. The minutes dragged on.

There were several monitors, most of which were on, and a few more were being turned on and checked. Soon the re-entry maneuvers were in play and the shuttle was in the burn no-communication portion of the flight. All ears were fastened on the communication link that was broadcast throughout the facility. There was great concern that the shuttle would burn up during this phase of the operation. It was exasperating. Several of the men who seemed to be running the show were starting to fidget. Their nervousness was evident, and one muttered to the other something about the procedure taking too long.

The base commander cued the com-link. "Anything from the planes - - - anything at all from any planes - - - talk to me - - - somebody - - -

- - anything - - - report." The foreboding silence returned. Someone rushed up to the base commander and quietly said, "They're nearly a minute over contact time."

Ten charged seconds later one of the high-altitude tracking jets cut in, "I have them in view - - - am moving closer." The shuttle crew's commander faintly tagged in through the jet's radio.

"It got really hot in here - - - think it fried some of our radio capability. The jet is close enough that we're bleeding over onto his radio signal. We don't have very much range, so pilot, please stay close."

Everyone on the ground listened intently. The first set of chutes was already gone and they were on the second. System failure warnings were tripping one after another. The base commander was shaking his head slowly and mouthed the words "too fast." Chute set number two ripped away, and the third and final set was deployed. If it didn't stay together for a little while, they would likely miss the runway altogether.

"Forty seconds, and the third chute is still holding," reported the flight coordinator.

"Son, you're coming in hot, but on track."

"The catch-net vehicles are rolling."

"Stay on center stripe."

When the shuttle tires first hit the runway, it was traveling over three hundred miles an hour, well above their spec ratings. All catch-net trucks were rolling at their top speed. The shuttle missed the first set of catch nets completely and was closing rapidly on the second. The right side rear tires blew at about the same time the shuttle hit the second set of catch nets. The drag chutes affixed to the catch nets immediately deployed and were forcefully pulled along down the runway by the speeding shuttle.

The shuttle twisted to the right as the right side landing gear collapsed. It then caught the third set of catch nets. They too were ripped from their vehicles and their drag chutes also deployed. This added additional drag and also added to the surreal picture that was being monitored from a dozen different cameras. In a few more seconds, all the remaining landing gears assemblies on the shuttle collapsed. The shuttle lowered to the runway and rapidly skidded down the runway slightly askew, with sparks flying profusely. As spectacular as it was visually, it was just as spectacular audibly. The sound was mind-searing as the underside of the shuttle was ground off by the massive weight it carried.

Near the end of the runway the shuttle came to a stop. It was likely that as much as 30 percent of the front underside was gone. There was no fire, but there was considerable smoke. Attempts to reach the shuttle crew by radio were unsuccessful. Rescue vehicles raced to the scene.

At this point, Darren and Paula were not allowed to go to the recovery site. Their view, especially with all the cameras and monitors in use, couldn't be better. The shuttle crew was alive, but all were suffering from heat-related complications. The crew members, one-by-one were quickly extricated from the scene as specialists moved in to report on the condition of the cylinder. It did not appear to be damaged, but much of what was left of the shuttle would have to be destroyed just to get the cylinder out. Since the shuttle was already totaled, the point was moot.

In order to hide the cylinder extraction procedure, a high wall of industrial fabric was quickly erected around and over the entire wreckage area. Any curious eyes attempting to see what was going on, even from a satellite would be prevented from doing so. After waiting for the additional cover of darkness, a hundred-ton portable crane was brought in to free the cylinder from the shuttle. Once lifted, it was immediately loaded onto an oversized flatbed truck and taken to the maintenance hangar at the far end of the runway.

As the media team waited for the go-ahead to move to the observation area, they watched some of the national news reports. A commentator was reporting on the emergency shuttle landing, explaining that the shuttle was forced to land at White Sands due to a minor problem with the navigation system. Damage was reportedly minimal, and the shuttle was expected to be made operational after some minor refurbishing.

"Yeah, right," muttered Paula, as she passed the monitor and headed for the hangar.

The short ride to the hangar on the runway shuttle was bumpy. The desert winds which were usually calm at this time of the night were still blowing. Hurrying out of the brisk wind and entering the hangar proved to be startling and almost surreal. Several high-intensity-metal-halide lights surrounded the specially prepared work area.

Electronic instruments of every kind and assorted configuration had been assembled in anticipation of every imagined contingency.

Cutting equipment, forklifts, armed military, and a team of technicians wearing protective suits stood ready. Some of the technicians had already attached a number of leads to the cylinder to monitor it and test its composition. Two analysts within earshot of Darren and Paula were discussing some of the data they had received.

"I don't know what it is, but it appears to be a combination of metal and plastic in solution." said the first technician to the second. "And the magnetic readings I'm getting are just about off the charts. Maybe that's got something to do with why the darn the thing is so heavy."

Darren and Paula found Stan working on his laptop, seated in what appeared to be the data management area. They headed directly for him. About halfway across the hangar, the equipment monitoring the hull energy readings began sounding alarms, and lights started flashing. Energy-reading monitors were tracking a slow and steady increase. A voice over the PA system ordered everyone to evacuate the primary work area.

The surface of the cylinder began to emit a bluish-green aura. At the midway point of the cylinder, a crosswise seam appeared where a few moments before there had been none. It continued to widen until an opening about twelve feet long and five feet wide appeared.

Ten seconds after opening, the darkness within the cylinder was replaced by a strange pink glow. Then everything stopped and an uneasy quiet filled the hangar. Slowly, one by one, everyone who just a few moments before had been fleeing from the object began to approach the cylinder again. Curiosity was overcoming fear as the more senior members of the team reached the cylinder first.

Chapter 7

Small Beginnings

Dr. Richard Tillman, one of the brightest members of the retrieval team, was among the group that first looked inside the cylinder. Behind a sheet of glasslike material and suspended in a slightly luminescent pink liquid was what appeared to be a man. Tubes were attached to his mouth, nose, and abdomen. He was pale-skinned and a little stockier than the norm but otherwise looked like a man, down to those clearly visible attributes that identify gender.

A battery of dials and instruments identified by indistinguishable markings filled the craft's compartment area. In slow motion, and compelled by the wonder of the moment, the doctor stretched his arm into the compartment area. Triggered by his hand's intrusion into the compartment, a repeating chiming sound began, and the liquid surrounding the unconscious body began to disappear. The tubes attached to the body retracted, and the body slumped to the bottom of the compartment as the last of the liquid was drawn off. The glasslike door of the compartment slid aside, and the limp body started to move ever so slightly. It seemed as if he was trying to cough as the faint contractions in his chest and abdomen intensified.

While most of the onlookers stood in shock, Dr. Tillman commanded the team into action. "Get him out of there! He can't breathe!"

The still unconscious but slightly convulsing figure was quickly taken out of the compartment and placed on a worktable. Wasting little time, Dr. Tillman directed that the body be positioned so the liquid that remained in the upper portion of the respiratory cavity could run out - - - standard procedure for a near drowning victim. Within minutes, the man, or alien, or whatever it was, maintained a labored breathing pattern. His pulse was strengthening.

Darren and Paula finally looked away from the scene and at each other. Paula sought Darren's confirmation on what she thought she was seeing. "An alien?"

Darren, also stunned, whispered back. "It sure looks like it!"

What followed was confusing. The reporters tried to pay attention, but the questions in their own minds made following the details difficult. Still, they got the gist of it. Lieutenant Stevens was already in the "inform and debrief mode" with them. With IV bags, a portable EKG, and other monitoring devices attached, the alien, now looking more like a patient emerging from major surgery, was wheeled to a more appropriate room. The media team was politely and discreetly escorted back to their motel room. Supposedly, the medical staff had determined that the alien needed rest and life support until his condition was stabilized.

***

Standing in front of the motel, Darren and Paula watched Stevens drive off. Something wasn't right.

"Are you feeling what I'm feeling?" questioned Paula.

"Yeah, I think we just went from in the loop to out in the cold."

Paula, the once little girl who worried about how her ears looked, and Darren who survived the belittling comments of an immature high school football coach, were on the verge of breaking the biggest story in modern history. Still, the recent turn of events stung sharply.

Inside the White Sands café, the two abandoned reporters tried to smother their irritation over their eviction with late-night desserts. Paula had already eaten the better part of a slice of key-lime pie and began sampling the strawberry shortcake. Darren alternated between his brownie fudge cake and bites of Paula's shortcake.

"What in the hell happened?" Darren moaned.

Annoyed by his occasional use of what she called "trash talk," Paula shot him a look that let him know she was not thrilled with his word choice. "Well, the first problem I see is that you're letting your hurt feelings get hold of your tongue. To your question, you're right, something happened. We pretty much got kicked out of there." They continued to lick their wounds, trying to figure out who was responsible and why they had been so abruptly dismissed.

"I have to admit, I'm so aggravated about being squeezed out that I'm tempted to get on the phone and tell everyone we know about this thing. This is huge!" Darren said.

"Yeah, everything we were told in journalism school about staying composed and not becoming emotionally involved is getting a workout," Paula said. "I feel like I'm about ready to explode - - - and you're right. It's about all I can do to keep from calling my parents and all of my friends, but that little session we had with the general is still fresh enough in my mind that doing something like that doesn't sound like a good idea either."

They hadn't noticed that Stan had entered the café. He came directly to their table and sat down. It was obvious Stan was rushed and not there to make small talk. He looked around the dining area to make sure no one was within earshot.

Stan hunched forward and began a two-minute monologue. "Look, I wanted to catch up with you, but I couldn't get away until now. I saw you get escorted out, and that's when some of the chatter I'd been hearing started to make sense." The two were speechless and soaked up every word.

Stan continued. "Prior to what we all saw a few hours ago, everyone thought we would be retrieving and examining some kind of artifact. We considered the prospect of finding life on board, but only as an extremely remote possibility. We were more prepared for object analysis—not for what we got.

"Some of the chatter started just after the cylinder came into orbit, and it really kicked in after we opened it. Let's just say that given the new direction things have taken, a certain element in the military doesn't see this as a great opportunity for scientific advancement. The Department of Defense sees this as a possible scouting mission for an alien invasion."

Paula and Darren's eyes widened even more.

"Invasion!" Paula blurted.

"You've got it," replied Stan. "I think that's all hogwash, and we're on the verge of blowing one of the greatest opportunities any one of us will see in our lifetime. I'm not ultra military minded; I came up more in the nerd ranks, but some of the military geniuses' think we ought to dissect the ship and the occupant - - - you know, learn all we can before the invasion."

"Nutso," breathed Darren.

"Exactly," said Stan as he rose to leave. "I don't want to be gone too long. I need to get back, but I wanted to let you know what was going on. Just be cool with it and see how they come back to you. But don't push. I'll let you know what I can, when I can.

"Oh, and another thing. If this thing goes south, you might want to become invisible till it blows over." With that said, Stan turned and walked out of the café.

Paula and Darren stared at one another. Paula spoke first. "Invasion?"

Darren responded in the same hushed voice. "You heard the man—invasion! I think calling it PMS for Paranoid Military Supposition would be a little closer to the mark."

***

The following morning, Lieutenant Stevens called, supposedly to give the reporters an update, but it felt more like an attempt to patch up the fallout from their abrupt dismissal the night before. Maybe they were a little overly suspicious because of what Stan had told them, but they were proceeding with caution nonetheless. Stevens invited them back to the facility. It seemed someone was trying to win back their confidence and cooperation. Just who it was, they weren't sure, but to Darren it smelled as if someone other than General Adams was pulling these new "invasion" strings. Adams seemed hard-nosed but straight up, someone whose word you could count on.

Upon returning to the base, Paula was especially amazed at the transformation that had taken place. The shuttle and any trace of the wreckage recovery effort were gone. Everything at the gate appeared Base Normal, except for the additional armed personnel stationed at the gate. Whisked through the entry point, they returned to the maintenance hangar. Guards again checked their IDs outside the hangar, and they were allowed to enter.

Stevens escorted them into the main hangar area. Centered and suspended by straps was the cylinder. It had been cleaned, and it gleamed under the intense metal-halide lights. The gaping hole that had been opened to allow access was now closed. No cracks were visible; it appeared to be one seamless, highly polished steel cylinder. It had the reflective quality of a huge drop of mercury. Sensing the question in their minds, Stevens answered, "No, we didn't close it up. It just closed up by itself last night, and we haven't figured out how to get it back open again." Several technicians were at work around the craft. A number of tests appeared to be in progress.

Stevens made a quick stop at the craft analysis center and asked the technician in charge, "Anything new?"

"No, nothing yet," responded the head technician. "Can't cut it. Laser just bounces off—ultrasound, heat, nothing."

Stevens then took Paula and Darren to a room in the administrative area of the building not far from where the alien had been taken to recover. Several minutes later, Stan entered the room with a sunglass-wearing associate who looked like he was Special-Ops. Stan behaved coolly toward the reporters, an obvious signal that he wanted to avoid the perception of friendship between them. His demeanor conveyed potential danger.

"I have some information for you to bring you up to speed," Stan said. "T-1 - - - that's what we're calling him for now; it stands for Traveler One, is recovering and even speaking. We have some linguistic experts working with him right now.

"He has his own language, which he occasionally slips back into, and he's definitely not from around here. The linguistic experts are amazed at how fast he is starting to pick up our words and communicate with us.

"Initial tests indicate that he comes from a planet that has a much greater field of gravity than Earth's. We still aren't sure what the craft is composed of, but his physical composition is only slightly different from our own. He's used to gravity over twice the force of Earth's. To enable him to move as he is accustomed to, we've designed a set of weights that approximate his normal gravity. You'll be allowed to see him in a few minutes. He says his name is something like Ana-key-toes Ash-kan-az-a. So, to make it easy on everyone, we're using T-1. He seems to respond well to that.

"Now for the more clinical information: The weight belts around his waist, wrist, ankles, and neck are necessary to maintain his equilibrium and balance. He's 5-foot-11, weighs 289 pounds, and is wearing a little over 300 pounds of weight to help correct for gravity. He is pleasant, ambulatory, and interacting with the technicians and lab personnel that have been working with him. When you do visit him, make sure you don't get caught between him and a wall as he's moving around. He's still getting used to our gravity and the belts and all, and he's still a little bit wobbly. If he accidentally bumps into you, you could get hurt. Just be careful. Any questions?"

Chapter 8

Friend or Foe?

The analysis team had been careful about introducing new personnel to T-1. They were curious to see how he would react to Paula, the first Earth female he would see. Darren entered first. His heart raced as he made his way into the containment room. T-1 was sitting on a hospital bed. He was engaged in playful dialogue with three attendants and listened intently whenever one of them spoke. With concentrated effort, he responded in rough, broken English. He sounded like a Russian who had been exposed to very little English.

T-1 was wearing a pair of knee-length, loose-fitting workout shorts and a loose-fitting sweatshirt with the sleeves cut back to the elbow. The strap-on weights were visible and probably the reason for the loose-fitting attire. The weight units were made of heavy-duty nylon fabric filled with a heavy material to provide more weight. Heavy-duty, double-wrapped Velcro straps secured the weight material in position. Had Darren not known about the actual weight involved, T-1 wouldn't look much different from any of the beefed-up workout fanatics who frequented the weight rooms at the fitness club he belonged to. Whether he was speaking or listening, T-1 wore a childlike smile and exhibited a pleasant demeanor.

T-1 noticed Darren only after his cautious approach brought him within ten feet of the bed. He then turned to focus his attention on Darren. T-1's facial expression was friendly and inviting. He seemed eager to meet this new person, since he had become accustomed to the team of six technicians he had been working with. "Day-a-Run" was his first attempt at saying "Darren." T-1 kept repeating it and got marginally better.

In another few minutes, Paula was allowed into the room, with the same slow-approach instructions. This time there was a noticeable difference in T-1's reaction. He instantly began to straighten himself and seemed more self-conscious of his appearance than he had been before. His thick fingers brushed at his coarse raven-black hair a time or two. Apparently, he had noticed the differences in the female of the human species. It seemed he was trying to make a good impression. "Paul-Ah" was T-1's first shot at Paula's name, and it never much deviated from that. The visit was relatively short, but Paula and Darren were grateful that they had been allowed to meet the first alien ever known to officially arrive on planet Earth.

In the next three-day period, Darren and Paula were allowed three separate visits with T-1, each visit lasting longer than the previous one. T-1's command of English improved somewhat but then started to level off. Though no one was absolutely sure, it appeared that T-1 was from a planet circling Beta Canum Venaticorum some twenty-six light-years away. Communication was limited, since T-1 and the humans shared no common root languages. But it seemed that T-1 was on a mission to find life on a planet other than his own.

Earth's search for life had consisted of listening for detectable life-sign emissions from a broad spectrum of possible habi-stars. These stars were chosen from a pre-selected list of possibly life-supporting target stars as part of Earth's planned launch of the Terrestrial Planet Finder probe. T-1's scientists had carried their project much further than Earth's had. T-1 was part of a long-range plan consisting of seven manned probes that were sent out to their pre-selected life-sign target solar systems.

On their third visit, the journalists got a chance to see an unusual part of T-1's health and conditioning program. He was given a forty-five-minute workout regimen that included rigorous cardio training with his 300-pound weight suit on, and then ten minutes with the weights off. When he took the belts off, T-1 began jumping up and down like a teenager on a trampoline; only he was doing this from a solid concrete floor. He kept jumping higher and higher which was reminiscent of the way astronauts jumped on the moon's surface, but without the slow-motion effect. T-1's first few jumps sent him almost twenty feet into the air. After he landed he paused, focused, and exerted himself again. He soared more than twenty-five feet straight up and grabbed the steel crossbeams on the hangar ceiling. He held on and swung there for a few seconds, then released his hands and landed heavily on the floor, but without apparent injury.

Paula overheard one of T-1's workout coordinators. "It's amazing what he can do. When you consider he has the speed, mobility, and strength of a pro-football linebacker, and that's all while he's wearing over 300 pounds of weight! Well, I wouldn't want to be part of a street gang that might try to mug him in a dark alley, especially with the weight belts off. It wouldn't be pretty."

Having extensively measured and monitored T-1's workouts, the training crew had a healthy sense of fear and respect for the alien. The gentle visitor from another world had the strength of a full-grown mountain gorilla.

"You see that little scar on T-1's left forearm?" a technician asked. "Well, that happened yesterday when T-1 was exercising in the hangar and bumped into one of the side support beams. He hit something sharp, and it gave him a pretty healthy cut that bled a good bit. They decided to med-tape it together rather than stitch it up. It looks like it's healing pretty fast.

"The point is, even though his speed and strength far surpasses that of humans, he still can bleed and get hurt if we don't keep a close eye on him. That's why all the interior side beams now have padding around them. We don't want the number one visitor on the planet accidentally breaking something. It's not like we can run him over to the local hospital and give him a transfusion or something. We don't exactly have alien blood in the blood bank."

From a number of sources, Darren began organizing what would certainly have to be the most sensational story of the millennia—that is, if it ever got the OK to release it. Between what Stan confided, what the technicians provided, and what T-1 struggled to convey in a number of subsequent conversations, the story unfolded: He was comparable to one of our astronauts, selected after surviving a rigorous elimination process. The twenty-six light-year trip to Earth took about a hundred Earth years to complete. Before leaving his planet, he had been placed in a state of suspended animation inside the pink life-supporting liquid. Most likely everyone T-1 knew back on his home planet had died by now.

Using their newly developed cross magnetic field propulsion system, T-1's colleagues back on his home planet were able to attain a space constant speed of around a quarter of the speed of light, which by Earth standards was quite a feat. The cross magnetic field drive was also the reason so much cosmic debris had latched onto and followed the craft. In Earth time, it took his craft nearly two weeks to reach that speed and a similar amount of time to reverse thrust and decelerate again.

Sensors on the craft were designed to seek out the energy signals of any civilization advanced enough to be using communication technology. Then the craft could home in on the signals and orbit the technologically advanced planet at the center of the activity.

T-1 was like a sponge when it came to finding out about Earth's culture and society. He would ask a question about Earth, and someone on the team would give an answer. Then someone on the team would ask him about his world, and he would give his answer, the best he could give the speech barrier. Though these sessions were a joy to witness and participate in, the reporters realized something was changing. Exactly when and how it crept in didn't really matter, though everyone involved could see and feel the effects.

Around the fifth day, each side of this cultural exchange started getting a little suspicious of the other side. The suspicion likely crept in when they became curious about conflict and war on each other's planet. The technicians were curious about their weapons, and T-1 was equally curious about Earth's technology. The military brass behind the one-way glass of the observation room started getting paranoid when the conversation touched on the military. T-1's superior strength and the cylinder's ability to resist access didn't help.

Gradually, the free and open flow of information became more guarded. The military started feeling that T-1 was hiding something, and T-1 had to feel that the technicians' answers were becoming less than candid. Darren and Paula watched the warm and friendly visits transform into more of an interrogation. On day seven it wasn't much fun anymore. It wasn't a big surprise when Stevens informed them that T-1 was going to be moved into another phase of the program and that their daily visits would be on hold until further notice. The ride back to the motel was overshadowed by an ominous feeling. An opportunity of a lifetime was slipping away from them.

Shortly after they reached the motel, Stan called Paula on her cell phone. His voice sounded icy, impersonal. Paula picked up on his unspoken warning.

"Paula, this is Stan from the base. I just wanted to return the sun glasses you left here today." Since Paula had her sun glasses in her hands, she knew Stan was concerned about who else might be listening. Stan continued. "I'm going to catch dinner over at the café across the street from your motel, if you want to come by."

Paula followed his lead. "Sure, I can do that—you're right, I don't have them. Are you going there right now?"

"Yes, I should be there in about five minutes. I only have time to eat and run, so if you want to run over and pick them up—"

"Good, - - - good, that would be great. OK then, see you in five minutes." Paula finished and hung up. She looked over at Darren, who was giving her a "what's going on?" look. "Something's up!" Paula said. "Stan wants to meet us in five minutes at the diner, and he sounds - - we've got to go - - hurry!"

Stan was already seated at the booth closest to the bathrooms and the farthest table from any other customers in the diner. Stan started quietly talking the minute they sat down. "I've only got about three minutes, so pay attention. You're both sharp, and you can probably see a good bit of what's going on, but it's even worse. That invasion mentality I mentioned before, well, it's kicked up a notch. Seems the advisers around the president have him all but convinced that T-1's an alien scout and we need to rip his ship apart and figure out everything we can about their technology. Here's the worst part."

Stan held his hand up with his thumb and index finger practically touching. "They're about this far from giving the order to dissect T-1 and learn everything out about his physical makeup so we can use biological weapons on them in the quote, big invasion." Stan looked at their wide-eyed wonder and then continued. "They're even talking about what kind of torture methods to use on him since they think he knows a lot more about weapons and technology than he's admitted to."

In semi-disbelief Darren questioned, "Torture?"

"That's right, I know, today's new more friendly military's not supposed to do that anymore, right. But you're forgetting, T-1 is not human. Way before you could argue the point the damage would be done; and, remember, none of this is public knowledge. As crazy as it sounds, the anti-invasion plan seems to be coming down to torture him till they're satisfied that there is no more information they can obtain, and then dissect and analyze his body to find any physical weaknesses in his body that might give the military some kind of edge."

The drained expressions on Darren and Paula's faces momentarily masked the inner anger that was welling up inside.

Before they could say anything Stan continued. "Don't even try to talk, just listen. There's this paranoid Department of Defense agent named Kendall Frank who is stirring this poison, but its probably best not to get me started."

Stan pulled four cell phones in a plastic zip lock bag out of his briefcase and slid them across the table. "Take these and this list of numbers for four other phones that I have. These are prepaid cell phones I picked up just in case. Don't use your phones to call my cell or even my home phone. Use these if you need to call me, and keep switching the ones you use. That'll make it harder to trace and follow. This could get serious, no, it is serious. I know these types, and they can get wacko. Watch yourself. Be as low-profile as you can. Don't trust anybody! I'll call when I can."

Just like that, Stan stood up and headed for the door. He never looked back.

Chapter 9

Albuquerque Turkey

Two uneventful days passed as the couple tried to tough it out. The separate room arrangements were working well, yet they were getting a little stir crazy just hanging around the motel and diner waiting for something to happen.

The next morning while Darren was still resting in his room, Paula took the vehicle and made a run to the store. The enormity of the event had been pressing in on her. She wanted to tell someone about T-1, but her professional ethics and her concern about the panic that could result kept her quiet. Still, she felt a growing temptation to share the experience with the two most influential people in her life, her parents.

Before reason talked her out of it, she picked up her phone to make the call. She considered using one of Stan's prepaid phones, but her parents didn't answer calls from unfamiliar numbers. She was taking a risk, but reason was not completely in charge. As she waited for someone to answer, she wondered, *What are the chances that a call to my parents in a small Nebraska town would create a problem?*

The ringing stopped when her mother answered the phone. "Paula, where on Earth have you been? Are you OK?"

"I'm OK, just been really busy. I'm sorry I didn't call sooner."

"Your father and I were starting to get worried. The station said you were in the field on assignment, and we didn't want to interrupt you or catch you at a bad time. But we were about ready to call you."

"I know. You're right. I should have called. My bad. So, how are you guys doing? How's Dad's blood pressure?"

"Well, you know your dad. He doesn't listen to what the doctors say, and he still uses too much salt. And whenever I give him trouble about his eating habits he gets irritated and pouts till I leave him alone. He's out in the garage if you want me to get him."

"No, Mom, I'm really short on time, but I just wanted to let you know that I'm working on something important, and I don't have time to get into the details. I wouldn't be here if it wasn't for you helping me get through college. I've been thinking about that a lot lately."

"Have you been going to church, staying close with God? Are you still seeing that reporter Darrel, or whatever his name is?"

Paula corrected what she knew to be her Mom's intended humor at mis-remembering Darren's name. "Now, Mom, you know perfectly well that his name is Darren. And to answer your next question, nothing *funny* is going on—and no, we're not planning to get married any time soon."

"Just make sure he's the one God's got picked out for you, that's all your father and I want. Just for you to be happy and for you to be where God wants you to be."

"I don't have everything figured out, but right now I'm certain that I'm where God wants me to be."

Not wanting to be on the phone longer than necessary, Paula finished the call and hoped she wouldn't regret using her own personal cell phone. She could almost feel the governmental scrutiny like an invisible cloud that hovered in the shadows. She hadn't revealed anything about the story, but

Paula could still feel the general's stiff words of warning. With her mission accomplished, she returned to the motel breakfast room and found Darren there indulging in the free continental breakfast bar. She joined him and made no mention of the call to her mother.

Darren had been thinking through this new challenge, and began telling Paula about a lifelong friend named Kurt who lived less that a hundred miles north in Albuquerque. Kurt, he said, had frequently asked Darren to visit him. Darren believed this was the opportune time for that visit and Paula agreed.

Using one of the prepaid phones, Darren called Kurt and made plans for a visit. Paula used her regular cell phone to tell Stevens that they would be sightseeing in the mountains for a few days and could be reached on their cell phones. Before Stevens could figure out how to respond, Paula hung up. They were free, as least for a while.

Darren was hoping for a calming, relaxing drive through the mountains, but it didn't turn out that way.

"So, how does this fit into God and the Bible and everything? I mean, how does the Bible explain aliens - - - or how do you explain what the Bible has to say about aliens?" Darren asked.

He ventured on into dangerous territory—Paula's solid, faith-saturated turf. Before Paula could answer, he continued. "Now, I just don't remember too much in the Bible about aliens."

Paula tensed a little as she sensed a hint of "maybe this proves the Bible's wrong" in Darren's voice. She stood her ground. "I'm not the biblical scholar that I should be, granted."

"From where I am you sure are."

"I'm just saying I don't know that there is anything in the Bible that definitively says there are aliens out there or says that there are not."

Darren pushed. "Well, it seems to me that when the news of T-1 gets out, a whole lot of people on Earth are going have a real crisis of faith. What will the pope say? What about all those preachers preaching hellfire and brimstone? Where do aliens fit in? They might have a real problem. I mean, I know you're into the God thing way more than me, but they're going to have a problem explaining why God forgot to mention anything about aliens."

Paula calmed herself. "Well, you're right—we're not on the same page on the God thing, that's for sure." Darren felt a sharp pain as he realized he'd pretty well destroyed any hope that this would be the day he'd pop the question. He readied himself for what he had invited.

"That's why I'm relieved we haven't let things get too serious between us," she said. Darren's left hand, the one holding the ring in his pocket went hot and sweaty. Paula continued. "And who knows? Maybe you'll get serious about God one day, but I'm not all worried about that right now. That's between you and God. And this T-1 thing, I just don't know. But I'm not going to get all bent out of shape over it. I'm going to trust God and know that He's not surprised or shaken by T-1 or a thousand T-1s. Like my old pastor used to say, 'When all's been said, and all's been done, evil will falter, and God will have won.'

The conversation had become adversarial in tone, not Darren's intention. He tried to recover, but not with the result he imagined. "OK, I'm not trying to stir up anything, but it's just that you are a lot more outspoken about your beliefs, and you know, there are a lot of people who believe that your religion or your beliefs are a personal thing, that it's between you and God," he said.

Paula answered with calm conviction. "You know, I used to think like that. Then one day I heard a preacher give a sermon about just what you are saying. He talked about how so many professing Christians have that 'keep your Christianity to yourself' mindset and how that attitude really comes from the mouth of the enemy. He talked about how these professing Christians are afraid to offend somebody by bringing up their faith. He said that often these are good, hard-working people who do good works but are reluctant to speak openly and directly to others about their need of Christ. Then the preacher said something like, 'Hell is full of people who somebody was afraid to offend.' Think about that! I sure did."

Paula's eyes locked on Darren's. "The preacher went on to say that many Christians feel they don't know enough about the Bible, or they don't feel comfortable intruding into someone else's life. The truth is, he said, more often than not they are in some part ashamed and a little embarrassed about being associated with this 'turn the other cheek' Jesus. But Jesus said, '*Whoever* denies Me before men, him I will also deny before My Father who is in heaven.' Just failing to speak up for Jesus when we have a chance to do so is denying Him."

Darren was reluctant to say anything, so Paula continued. "Our words are a major part of the doorway that leads to eternal life. There's an old Italian proverb that says 'Silence is consent.' It means that when we are silent, when we should speak up in the interest and benefit of others, the blame, in part, becomes our own. Many Christians are too tongue-tied to speak up about their faith, thinking their good deeds are enough. The devil couldn't be happier."

Darren interjected, "Well, I always thought that doing good to others was probably good enough."

Paula responded, "Sure, it's important to do good things for other people and to show compassion for them. And who knows? Maybe they'll even ask why you do those things, and you can tell them about Jesus. God has given every believer 'the Words of life,' and we aren't supposed to keep them to ourselves. We should always be ready to tell others about Jesus. The people we love may spend eternity apart from God because we as *Christians* are too ashamed, or better, too intimidated to speak up for our faith."

She continued, "That preacher also talked about how a lot of professing Christians aren't really what they're professing to be. He used the acronym CINO which he said meant, 'Christians In Name Only'. This means that because they belong to a certain denomination or attend church, they think they are "saved" enough. He said that a good indicator that someone might be *really* *"saved"* and in an acceptable relationship with the Lord is that they have a respect for, a desire for, and they are actively pursuing the Word of God. He said it's just about impossible for someone to have a real love for God and to live as God wants us to live, and at the same time have a disinterest in His Word. After all, Jesus is named and bears the title of "The (living) Word of God".

"The pastor said the other characteristic that's a key indicator that someone might really be "saved", was whether they were putting forth effort to help others come to a saving knowledge of Jesus Christ. He said, people who are lost do not have their 'fear of God' working, and they do not realize the terrible danger they are in should they suddenly die. They are like someone blindfolded wandering around on the highway totally unaware of the trucks and cars that are soon to come. If we just stand around and do nothing to save them, we are held accountable. In essence he was saying that if someone isn't particularly interested in the Word of God, and they aren't actively concerned about and working to bring others to a saving knowledge of Christ, then one could easily question their salvation.

"The Word of God says, *"let a man examine himself"*, which we'd all be better off to do daily, especially in light of those two characteristics. When Jesus spoke about some of the people in His time, He said, '(They) *honor Me with their lips, but their heart is far from Me'*. When I heard this, it was a wake-up call for me and should be for all professing Christians today who may be deceiving only themselves."

"Wow - - - I didn't mean to go on like that" Paula said. - - - "I guess something must have hit a nerve. Anyway, that's just something to think about, and I know I need to do a better job on all this myself."

Darren finally spoke up. "No, everything you said makes sense. Now I'm sure I'm nowhere close to where you are." Darren tried to lighten the tone. "I mean, I don't think I'll be the guest speaker at church Sunday, if you know what I mean. But I was listening! I'm really thinking about it. - - - you know, - - - you said a lot."

Once again, Paula recognized Darren's tendency to avoid spiritual commitment, the one thing standing between him and God's plan for his life. The remainder of the trip was not exactly the warm, pre-engagement interlude that Darren had envisioned.

***

Finally, Darren and Paula arrived in Albuquerque. They checked into separate rooms at a motel near Kurt's house, paying by cash to stay under the radar.

For the first few days, good times and relaxation looked to be on the horizon. Kurt proved to be a warm host and a great guide to Albuquerque, which in turn proved to be a beautiful city. Life was starting to look good again to Darren.

But at 6 a.m. on his third day in the city, Darren, who had been sleeping soundly, heard an annoying, unfamiliar sound. It was one of the cell phones Stan had given them. When he realized that, he sprang into action.

Holy sh—! Stan was calling! But even more surprising, it wasn't Stan.

"Hello," answered Darren, trying to do the "I really was awake" thing.

"Day-Run, is this Day-Run?"

At first, Darren couldn't believe what he was hearing. "T-1, is that you? T-1, is that you, T-1?"

"Day-Run, Stan make me call to you. He make me take away from building place. He make tell me to call and how use trans-talk phone. He say you help hide to me."

Darren was stunned. "Where are you? T-1, where exactly are you?"

T-1 responded, "Stan friend and escape me. He say tell you come to train house. I wait in train bar."

"Do you mean train car? Do you mean a train car?"

"Yes, in train kar. You come fast. Some try hurt T-1 from Stan, come fast." Click.

Darren's heart was pounding. He stood motionless. He slowly started to move, as if he was commanding himself to get going. He didn't fully understand what was going on, but he knew he had to get moving. He called Paula, jumbling up his hurried explanation. She sensed the urgency in Darren's voice and jumped into action. Ten minutes after the call, they were blazing down Interstate 25, heading south toward the White Sands airbase. Darren looked at his watch; 6:14 a.m. Speed: 94. Temperature: Didn't matter. The 230-mile, three-plus-hour trip took right at two and a half.

A little before nine o'clock they pulled into the railroad facility near Las Cruces, not far from the airbase. There was more air traffic than normal, as helicopters and several other military aircraft filled the skies. T-1's absence appeared to have been discovered, and all the stops had been pulled trying to find him. Darren retrieved the same phone T-1 had called on. He pushed the recall button and waited.

On the sixth ring, T-1 answered. "Hollow."

"T-1, this is Darren. I'm pulling into the train car area. Where are you?"

"Many box kar, I find you. How make me find you?"

"We are in a white Suburban, I mean, enclosed vehicle. I'll start moving around in a circle so you can see us."

"OK, I find." Click - - and T-1 was gone. After about five excruciating minutes of waiting and circling, suddenly, out of nowhere T-1 came trotting up next to their vehicle. Darren came to an abrupt stop, as did T-1. He just stood there as Darren and Paula waited for him to get in. In a few seconds, they realized T-1 didn't know how to use a car door. Darren jumped out and opened the rear door for him. T-1 tentatively climbed into the vehicle and fit himself into the seat. Darren jumped back into the driver's seat and sped off the railroad property. Police and law enforcement vehicles were beginning to saturate the area. Four minutes later, they were on the interstate and headed back in the direction of the only sanctuary Darren knew - - - Kurt's place.

Chapter 10

Ready, Set, Go!

Smooth might not be the best word to describe how the introduction of T-1 to Kurt went. In the relative safety of the RV travel trailer parked in Kurt's backyard, Darren made the formal introduction and told the story. Kurt thought it was a clever rendition of one of their childhood pranks of yesteryear, and he wasn't biting.

Darren directed a question to T-1. "T-1, please tell my friend where you're from."

T-1 hesitated and then answered, "Me T-1, born on planet call by name Ranar." Kurt listened and was trying to seriously weigh what he was hearing, but then he almost started to laugh. "Yeah, right."

Undaunted, Darren continued his effort to convince him. Kurt forced himself to remain attentive to Darren's logic. He started opening up slightly when he heard about the weight belts and could see them still secured on T-1. Darren and Paula were firing off, one after the other, giving a rushed recap of the events leading up to that minute. SkyFire was big news, and to Kurt, it was starting to look a little less like a prank. T-1 moved a little and accidentally broke the kitchen table in the RV where they were meeting. Kurt was no longer a total skeptic, but he still wasn't convinced.

Darren had an idea. Kurt had been a star football player in college and had an option to go pro when a knee injury redirected his career path. He stood six foot five and weighed around three hundred pounds himself. Darren led the group outside and instructed T-1 to remove the weight belts. He then had T-1 and Kurt face one another. He told Kurt to try to push his way through T-1. At first Kurt balked at the idea, but Darren's badgering got the best of him. He started off with a light push, but T-1 didn't budge. Darren told T-1 to hold his ground and not let Kurt push him back. Kurt kept turning up the heat, but T-1 was immovable. Kurt had broken a sweat and was getting mad, still, no movement.

With his point partially made, Darren stepped in and restructured the contest. He told T-1 that he was to push through Kurt and not to hold back. He told Kurt to likewise do whatever it took to stop T-1. T-1 looked a little apprehensive, but he made ready when Darren said, "Now I mean it T-1—this is important. Don't hesitate, and do it strong." With both male egos adequately prepped, Darren gave the "ready, set, go." Like two linemen on Super Bowl Sunday, they collided. T-1's hands thrust forward and caught Kurt in the chest. Kurt was lifted slightly, repelled and sent back about ten feet. He fell backwards and slid another five feet into a hedge bordering the backyard fence.

Darren rushed to Kurt who looked like a confused prize fighter who was trying to figure out how he ended up on the canvas and was struggling to get back on his feet. It took several minutes for Kurt to fully gather himself. Any doubt he had about T-1's authenticity was pretty well gone.

Since they needed to keep T-1's identity a secret, they decided to tell Kurt's children that T-1 was a friend of Darren and Paula's from Europe, which also explained his funny accent.

His cover story invented itself as Kurt introduced T-1 to the rest of his family. During the introductions, Kurt's wife Rene asked T-1 what he did for a living. Kurt jumped in and said he worked as a strong man in a circus. T-1 was pretty convincing, with the weight-belt attire back on and all. He resembled a professional weight lifter heading for a workout.

***

Back at the base, pandemonium was erupting. General Adams was digesting the tongue lashing he received from the Attorney General. The plans for the president to make a secret visit to the facility and meet T-1 might need to be changed. To facilitate the base visit, the president had planned to come a few days early for a visit to `the Albuquerque International Balloon Festival. Now they were forced to implement their original schedule and go to the festival the following weekend.

The Attorney General all but said that General Adams was at fault for letting the alien escape. The Attorney General hadn't been all that thrilled about the whole alien thing to begin with, and now he was firmly planted in the group with the "dissect him" mentality. Suddenly, every government entity that knew about the project was on full alert. The military was in constant communication with the White House. Likewise, the lines that once separated the Pentagon and key scientific personnel began to fade.

The escape was all the invasion fanatics needed. They rallied around their position, and it was a landslide after that. Fear squelched the voice of reason as the base leadership met to discuss the situation. Updates on the physical attributes of T-1 gave fear all the ammunition it needed. The report of T-1's ability to easily throw a hundred pounds a considerable distance, and to run at speeds of nearly fifty miles an hour when the weights were removed, quieted the closed-door congressional briefing. After watching the video footage of T-1 performing without the weights, the thought of an invading army of T-1s catapulted the "find him and dissect him" mentality.

The official line from Washington was "Catch him if you can; kill him if you must; don't let him get away; and don't let him near the ship."

The authorities were also awed by his ability to escape. Somehow, with no help - - at least as far as they knew - - T-1 had been able to slip past a number of security checkpoints and video monitors, and walk out of the facility undetected. Some were seriously considering the possibility that T-1 had concealed his ability to fly, since it seemed that he must have flown off into thin air. It would be some time before they suspected that a human was part of the escape plan. They would eventually start piecing it together, but for a short time T-1 was free to walk among humans on planet Earth.

Paula knew that they had to walk a fine line to avoid unwanted scrutiny. Since she had taken some acting classes, she volunteered to call Lieutenant Stevens to see when their next visit to the base and T-1 was scheduled. To make the call, they had driven back to within twenty miles of the base in case they were tracking her cell phone. It took a couple of minutes to get Lieutenant Stevens on the phone, but when she did, Paula would have made her acting coach proud.

"Lieutenant Stevens, this is Paula Roberts, just checking in."

Stevens responded with a somewhat tentative "OK."

"I was just calling to see when we can get another visit to the base. It's been several days, and even a short visit will help us maintain our story line."

"Just where are you?" Stevens asked.

"Oh, somewhere out in the mountains, doing a little sightseeing while we had a chance. But if there's an opening, we could be there in a half hour or so. Even just a short update." She whined slightly to make it sound as if they really wanted to make a visit.

Lieutenant Stevens said, "Hold on." He was obviously checking with someone else. Stevens came back on the line. "So what's the last you knew about the status here?" Playing dumb, Paula answered, "Status? Uh, well just that new phase you talked about, you know, with the research going on. Why, did we miss something? Are they moving the project? Do we need to relocate?" She was firing questions the way any reporter chasing the scent of a story would.

"No, no - - - hold on," Stevens stalled. More checking. Stevens was being coached by Agent Kendall. Kendall and the lieutenant had been in a meeting with General Adams, and Kendall had been hard-pressing the alien invasion paranoia.

Kendall whispered to Stevens, "Do you think she knows anything?"

With the phone silenced by his hand, Stevens shook his head and whispered to Kendall, "No, she's clueless."

Kendall then looked to Adams to get his confirmation.

"We have more important things to do right now than to visit with reporters!" Adams answered.

Kendall turned to Stevens and added, "Right now they're just an annoyance."

With the general on board, Kendall told Stevens, "Keep her - - keep the both of them out of here! Tell them we're tied up for a few days, that they won't be needed for several days. Tell them to keep sightseeing. The last thing we need right now is for this to leak to the media. Go! Go! Get them off the phone! And keep them the hell out of here!" Stevens, with a little more tact, relayed the message, and the couple was back on the road toward Albuquerque.

In the spirit of the surreal adventure that was unfolding, Darren leaned over and borrowed a bit of Hollywood history. "Toto, I don't think we're in Kansas anymore."

Chapter 11

Teddy Bears and County Fairs

Kurt and his family enjoyed the nice home that Kurt's computer consulting business provided. Kurt was a computer guru and had launched his own computer repair and maintenance business. He had a nice customer base that enabled him to support his family in relative comfort. It also paid for some of the toys Kurt had accumulated: three four-wheelers, a ski boat, and the latest addition, the forty-foot, fifth-wheel travel trailer that was now being used to hide an alien.

In private Kurt told his wife Rene, the real T-1 story. She too was skeptical, until Kurt removed his shirt and revealed the two large black-and-blue marks on his chest. They were mementos of a surreal turf war he'd had with T-1 and would be a convincing reminder to him for several days.

Kurt had a computer hooked up in the RV that he sometimes used for work. He showed T-1 how to use it, and the alien took to it remarkably well. He devoured all kinds of information about Earth and the history of humanity on the internet. Kurt calmed the apprehension both Darren and

Paula started to feel when T-1 lost himself in the information pipeline to the world. "It's cool, it's cool - - T-1's just like a kid who just found YouTube. It'll be OK."

After a day of T-1's near-constant surfing, Kurt, Darren, Paula, Rene, and the two children convinced him to tear himself away from the computer and go with them to the county fair. Reluctantly, T-1 agreed. They gave T-1 some money and briefly explained how to use it so he could, if necessary, blend in better.

Upon arriving at the fairgrounds, Kurt ran into one of his neighbors and set about introducing everyone. As the intros were being made, the eldest of the neighbor's children, a 16-year-old, stepped up to impress both his family and the group with his social skills. He moved a little closer to T-1, stuck out his hand, and said, "Hi, I'm Tony, and you're - - ?" Kurt's group tensed, ready to intervene if need be.

After a pause, and in classic T-1 style, T-1 responded, "Me Ray."

Kurt and company were dumbfounded.

"Ray?" Tony asked. "Ray what?"

More tensing among the group.

Then T-1 answered, "Rah-berts." No one was more startled by this name announcement than Paula.

Tony questioned, "Ray Roberts? Your name is Ray Roberts?" Tony went on, "That's cool! Are you from Arizona?" Unsure of how to respond, T-1 was tongue-tied.

Darren jumped to the rescue. "Yeah, I think he's part Indian or something." T-1 could have easily passed for being of Native American ancestry, with his rugged features, complexion, and dark, coarse hair.

When they got clear of their neighbors, they all broke out in laughter, except for T-1, or rather, Ray Roberts. When asked where he had come up with that name, he said that Ranar, his home planet, came to mind, and Ray just jumped into his head.

"And the 'Roberts', where did that come from?" asked Paula. T-1 explained that "it good last name to Paul-Ah, good last name to me too. Me not like T-1 too much now." So there it was. T-1, in a frantic mind search to come up with a first and last name, became Ray Roberts.

Throughout the evening the group started using T-1's self-appointed name of Ray. They were all getting into it, even Ray, until Kurt interjected the voice of caution. "Now I can understand why you like Paula's last name of Roberts, but using one of their last names might not be all that wise either. Maybe, as much as we all like the name Ray Roberts, we should consider something a little less likely to draw attention." The group concurred, with the exception of Ray.

"Me like Ray Rah-berts - - - think sound good - - - OK too," said Ray.

Paula explained that using her last name might somehow help the government to find him. She suggested that another common last name like Jones or Smith or Thomas might be better. Paula began cranking out names.

As Ray pondered the options given, he interrupted Paula and made a choice. "Me no like Joones-ah or Smith-ah - - me like Rah-berts better than other name to use. Ray Rah-berts sound like strong good name." That night T-1 became just Ray Roberts to his small group of friends. For all other intents and purposes, he would use the name Ray only. He never responded to T-1 after that.

The group was cruising the carnival midway when they came upon an arm-wrestling machine. Some of the local jocks were giving it a shot. Ray ambled closer and took interest. He had already proven his intelligence and ability to pick up on things easily, so no one in the group was surprised that he understood the mechanics of the game. He looked to Darren when the jocks were done.

"Ray want try to do?" he asked. Darren got some tokens and fed them into the machine. Ray's entourage watched curiously. Placing his hand in the grip of the mechanized arm, he waited. Suddenly, the machine engaged, and Ray's hand began to be moved with it. Sensing the challenge, Ray engaged. Watching what transpired from a distance, an arcade attendant got up to get an "out of order" sign to place on the now arm-dangling machine.

Several of the other spectators witnessing the match hurriedly shuffled their children away. Suddenly, Ray had become an intimidating presence. Realizing they were drawing too much attention, Kurt rallied the troops, and they continued on their tour of the carnival.

Paula understood that outings with Ray contained an element of risk, but the point was about to be driven home as they were leaving the fairgrounds. Ray had shown an interest in the animals he had been exposed to, and they likewise were drawn to him. The animals detected no fear or danger in him. He had interacted with a friendly golden Lab on the fairgrounds, and as they were waiting to cross the highway to the parking lot, the Lab ran out across the road. Sensing the danger the dog did not, Ray leaped onto the highway and toward the Lab, which was unknowingly trotting into the path of an oncoming pickup truck. Ray scooped up the Lab with his right arm, raised and bent his left arm in the direction of the truck, and braced for impact.

The driver of the pickup slammed on the brakes. The vehicle had slowed down to about twenty miles an hour when it made contact with Ray's braced and ready frame. The impact knocked Ray about ten feet back, where he stopped, still standing with the dog safely under his arm. Other cars were screeching to a halt as Ray relaxed from his defensive stance and casually walked back toward his group with the dog still held safely under his arm. The only visible result of the encounter with the truck was the slight limp that Ray walked off as he returned to the group.

He released the animal back to safety past the curb and simply explained, "Kar could hurt dog, Ray help dog." The front bumper of the pickup was bent, the hood buckled a good bit, and the airbags deployed. It was drivable, but the driver would be talking to his insurance adjuster. The real problem was all the attention from onlookers.

The driver of the pickup didn't help matters any. He came running over and kept going on and on about what he just saw. "That was unbelievable! Are you sure you're not hurt? I tried to stop but I couldn't! How did you do that?" Again, Kurt marshaled the group away from all the attention and toward the safety of the SUV.

As they eluded the growing group of on-lookers, Paula summed things up. "Well, I'd say that's just about enough excitement for one evening." Everyone agreed, except for Ray. It was as if he was in Disneyland and would have happily stayed at the fairgrounds all night if they had let him.

Lindsey, Kurt's 10-year-old daughter, wondered about the feat she had just seen.

"Daddy, could you do what Mr. Ray did?"

"Now darling, I know you think your dad can do just about anything, like most little girls do, right? Well, the truth is that daddy couldn't have done exactly what Ray did, because" - - Darren was waiting to hear this one - - "because, well, Ray is a well-trained" - - Kurt was thinking hard now - - "professional wrestler." Only because their faces were turned away from the children did the startled expressions on Darren and Paula's faces keep from ruining Kurt's attempt to obscure the facts a little.

"Yeah, honey, Ray's a big-time professional wrestler and comes from Europe - - - somewhere," added Rene.

"We go back fair now?" Ray asked.

Darren danced a little. "Well, maybe. Not tonight, but then again, maybe soon."

"Go back fair soon, Ray like go soon."

Darren mumbled under his breath, "Fat chance of that happening." He figured that only the humans in the group could have caught his sarcastic comment. What Darren did not realize was that Ray also had better-than-human hearing, and Ray fairly well understood the implication of Darren's comment. Ray was like a three-hundred pound sponge soaking up information from any available source.

At about that time Rene noticed a small cut on Ray's hand.

"Ray, you're hurt! There's a cut on your hand!"

Ray made light of it, saying, "Truck front scratch Ray hand. Ray be OK."

Ray concealed the minor-looking injury. His demeanor did not invite further scrutiny. The other occupants of the vehicle could not miss the "no more talk about hand injury" body language that Ray was conveying. No one pursued the subject.

Chapter 12

Come on Down

As part of its "Reach the City Crusade," Albuquerque's Freedom Church was holding an old-time tent revival at the edge of the fairground parking area. Pastor Russ was about three-fourths of the way through his sermon as the SUV slowly approached the tent entrance. Traffic in the parking lot had come to a standstill. With the windows in the SUV rolled down, the occupants could hear the message coming from inside the revival tent.

For a brief moment, the pastor's voice rose over the confusion of all the surrounding noise. "And I don't care what your political beliefs are, or whether you came from lots of money, or from a family with no money. It doesn't matter if you were born into wealth from Beverly Hills, or you have no parents and you're from Timbuktu, you need to make Jesus the Lord of your life." With that, Darren was ready to dismiss the religious blathering, but Ray suddenly got out of the vehicle and made a beeline into the revival tent. Darren immediately pulled over and stopped the SUV.

The stunned entourage quickly followed Ray into the service.

Pastor Russ, standing at a makeshift podium, addressed the small crowd seated on folding chairs. Ray listened for a few moments, then turned and slowly walked back out of the tent. He acted slightly distant; something he had seen or heard seemed to have initiated a distinct mood change. Deep in thought, Ray walked slowly back to the SUV, as did his friends.

Ray wasn't ordinarily what you would call talkative, but he was quieter than usual for the remainder of the trip home. With minimal small talk, Ray opted to "go sleep now" and disappeared into the seclusion of the travel trailer bedroom. A little more small talk, and Darren and Paula got ready to excuse themselves to return to the motel. It had been an exciting day and an even more exciting night. Even though everyone needed a good night's rest, the group stopped to assess. With Ray alone in the RV, and the rest of the group huddled in the privacy of Kurt and Rene's kitchen, Darren brought up what they all had noticed. "What was that all about?"

Paula chimed in. "Did you see the change in him? Everything was all exciting, and just like that he went cold."

"Yeah, the same kind of reaction that a lot of people get when all that religion stuff gets pushed on them," Darren added. He just had to be funny.

Paula started to give Darren "the look" again, but when they made eye contact, they both broke out laughing.

"No, really, Darren, something was different - - and I'm trying to be serious here."

"Yeah, I know," Darren answered. "Maybe we'll find out, maybe not. Maybe he just wasn't feeling good."

"Yeah, maybe it was getting hit by the truck, maybe he got hurt, and he wasn't letting on," Kurt suggested.

"Oh, I never thought of that," Paula said. "Everything was happening so fast. Breaking the arm-wrestling machine, saving the dog, walking into the tent meeting, and then his change in attitude."

"Did you notice that little limp he had right after the truck hit him? And the scratch on his hand?" Darren asked.

"Yeah, you're right - - he did limp for a few steps and then kind of shrugged it off. And he sure wasn't in any hurry to talk about that cut, or scratch, or whatever it was. He covered it up so fast," Paula said.

"You know, it just goes to show you that we are all a little caught up in his superhuman capability. It's easy to see him as a Superman, but he's not. Stronger than us, faster than us, yes, but these capabilities could easily get him hurt. What if that pick up truck had been a cement truck? You know, as soon as we got back, it almost seemed that he wanted to get away from us, to have a little distance."

Paula cut him off. "Don't even go there."

"What? I was only trying to - - - " Darren started.

Paula cut in again, "Yeah, I could almost smell where you were heading. Don't even think about Ray being some part of that invasion threat. Why, you saw what he did tonight. Jumped out and risked his life for a dog! And he's as gentle as a baby. He's not part of a great master invasion plot, and you know it!"

"Well, I don't know. How do we know for sure? I mean, as much as I like him, he scares me a little. Can you imagine if he decided he didn't want to be your friend? Yeah, you're right. We probably don't want to think about that."

Back at the RV, Ray was doing anything but sleeping. He was all over the Internet, frantically looking for something. Kurt's computer was set up so he could monitor the RV's computer activity from the office in his house. His girls occasionally had sleepovers in the RV, and he wanted to know if they were getting into things they shouldn't be. He never imagined that his security system would someday be used to monitor alien activities. But that night, Kurt slept soundly as Ray surfed the Internet.

In private conversations while away from Ray, Darren and Paula discussed the predicament they were in. Using another prepaid cell phone, Stan had filled in some of the blanks about what had happened and what was continuing to happen on the military side of things. Stan, for the time being, had been able to avoid scrutiny in Ray's escape. It probably wouldn't be too long before attention would turn in his direction, but he could dance with the best of them, especially when it came to technology and system interface. Stan had made it possible for Ray to seemingly vanish into thin air, and he had taken steps that would make it difficult to get a fix on his involvement.

The government, in its multifaceted form, was looking everywhere for T-1, or now Ray. Given the global situation, the national threat level was left at elevated, with no immediate plan to change it. Leads from every corner of the globe were being tracked down and systematically eliminated. They even tried to validate one report that the Russians had abducted him and were trying to align themselves with the aliens in advance of the coming "invasion."

About the only plan the group had to protect Ray was to keep him under wraps until the delusional mindset of the powers that be eased a little. Not a great plan, but for the time being, it was all they had. In the meantime, they wanted to expose Ray to the better side of humanity as much as possible, without detection. The reports of wild leads extending to faraway places gave them hope. It was a day-to-day thing. Every day they remained undiscovered was a mini-victory. Stan figured that at most, they had a few weeks. Either things would ease up, or they would get caught, and T-1 would fall victim to the flawed side of human understanding.

Stan's closing comment was this: "Don't travel a lot, blend in as best you can, and I'll let you know when and if things cool down."

Westhope, North Dakota

At a remote U.S.-Canada border station just north of Westhope, North Dakota, sworn enemies of the United States were in the process of implementing a carefully thought-out plan to bring America to her knees. This plan, designed and developed by Fahad's brother Ahmed, involved a very small group. Accompanied by two cousins, Ahmed prepared to enter the United States. Their flawless French passports and paperwork aroused little suspicion. After a brief interview and screening, they were allowed to enter. The three visitors stowed their bags in the rear of their waiting SUV and began their journey deep onto American soil. Not since 9/11 had so great a threat moved freely into the land of the again sleeping giant. The opportunity to strike at America, and at the same time undermine the Middle East peace initiative, was only a few days away.

Washington, DC

Air Force Major Angela Stutes waited in the ante-room of the threat assessment strategy session of the Pentagon. She herself had assembled much of the intel that was the basis of her report. Though no one else in her unit seemed to sense any encroaching danger in her information analysis, she knew something about this evaluation was different. And though the reports were curiously devoid of details, too many sources from around the globe were reporting a difficult-to-describe air of expectancy from within the anti-American terrorist network. She was apprehensive about running solo on this one, but something told her not to let this one go unreported.

When her moment arrived, she would muster the courage to at least push hard for an immediate elevation of the national threat level and state of preparedness. The loss of her sister in the 9/11 attack had made things personal, and she was well aware of her duty and the responsibility of her position. She was not going to chance any similar event on her watch. The door to the anteroom opened, she stood up, and entered the room ready to make her case.

Chapter 13

The Tide of All Humanity

Darren and Paula caught a little of the early morning news while having the continental breakfast at the motel. The recent historic change in the political structure of the Israeli government had laid the groundwork for the Middle East peace initiative to move forward.

Conditioned by their television station work clock, and also well charged by the enormity of the story they were in the midst of, Darren pulled into Kurt's driveway shortly before 7 a.m.. Walking back to the RV, they found Ray still glued to the computer with the cable TV running simultaneously in the background. Ray was searching the internet and was also sponging all the info he could off the TV. In a matter of a few days, he had joined the ranks of millions of media junkies on planet Earth.

But he also took a few detours. He spent some time watching cartoons and found them fascinating. He would belly laugh and go into uncontrollable fits of laughter at some of the simple slapstick antics he saw. He loved the Three

Stooges and had to force himself to return to his surfing.

Upon their arrival, Ray hurriedly cleared the screen and engaged with his visitors. The usual small talk followed. When asked how he was doing with his internet searches, he evaded the question and made a request. His English was slowly improving but was still a little rough. "We can go to fair now soon?" It was the first real request he had made. Since they had no other plans, Darren answered, "Why not?"

This trip it was just Ray, Darren, and Paula. They stopped to eat at Chick-fil-A, probably because Ray recognized their sign and made the connection. He pointed to the sign and said "EAT MORE CHIKIN?" Impressed with Ray's cognitive skills, eating there seemed in order. Obviously, Ray was learning about American culture through TV commercials. Ray really liked the two chicken sandwiches Darren ordered for him and asked for another. Ray liked the fries, the carbonated beverages, but the sandwiches he liked most of all. Ray was in his own fast-food heaven.

It was Wednesday early evening and there were only a few cars at the fairgrounds when they reached the parking lot. Darren and Paula began

146

heading across the street toward the midway, but Ray wasn't on the same page. Sensing his absence, they turned to see Ray heading back toward the revival tent. By the time they caught up with him, he was entering the Wednesday night service already in progress. Pastor Russ was at the pulpit again. Ray sat near the back and his escorts stood right behind him and listened to the pastor's message.

"Within the church too many people are all too comfortable, too controlled, and too complacent. They sit back and expect the pastors to do all the praying, and teaching, and comforting. This was not at all the plan Jesus had.

"Jesus did not send the disciples out to make good church members. He sent them out to make other disciples. In fact, He shared his life with a small group of men, His disciples. He turned over the entire responsibility of reaching the world to this small group of men. They were to then share their lives with others.

"In the Bible Jesus gave great insight into who would be part of His heavenly family and who would not. When told that His mother and brothers were waiting to see Him, Jesus explained that His real family, those who would be His eternal heavenly family, were those who do the will of His Father. The Father's will is for us to first come to accept Jesus as our Lord and Savior, and then to serve others as His Word tell us to. Father God's will for us is that we disciple or teach others, and teach them how to disciple others. If someone is not serving the Lord and not trying to help others accept Jesus, his or her inclusion in God's eternal presence in heaven is very much in question."

With several of the downtown area homeless people in attendance, Pastor Russ got very direct in his preaching. "The Bible says 'all have sinned and come short of the glory of God.' And that's why God sent His Son into the world, that through Him and His sacrifice on the cross, we might be forgiven of our sins and be saved."

The pastor continued, "You know, when Jesus allowed Himself to be slowly tortured to death for my sin, for your sin, in other words, for our self-centered, too-busy-for-God lives, Father God took that very seriously. In school, we learned about the three R's - - reading, writing and arithmetic. Today I want you to consider the three more important R's - - respect, regret, and rejoicing. Everyone who has lived, is living now, or will ever live, will spend all eternity either rejoicing or regretting. Everyone, even the most convinced atheist, will spend all eternity knowing and believing that Jesus is the Son of God.

"The question is, did they, while they were alive in this physical world, come to *respect* the great gift of God, the sacrifice that Jesus made? Rejoicing or regretting, respecting Jesus' sacrifice or not - - Father God looks on all creation through the cross of Jesus Christ.

"We must respect what Jesus did, even though we may not fully understand all that happened at the cross. If we ask for forgiveness and truly repent and turn away from our sins, God promises in His Word that He will forgive our selfish and sinful past, save us, and grant us eternal life with Him forever.

"If we hear about Jesus and aren't willing to accept Him and His sacrifice, neither will God accept us into His eternal presence. If we hear about Jesus and have the attitude, 'I'll get serious about God later, after I've had a chance to experience a little life first - - when I get older I'll do the God thing' - - sadly, that answer is still a no.

It's not a triple option: yes, no, or later. Once we've had a chance to hear about Jesus and God's plan to save us, we either say 'Yes, Lord,' like I did years ago, or we say no. Either we allow Jesus' sacrifice to change our lives, or we continue on with our own self-centered lives. God won't drag us into heaven, but He has made a way for us through Jesus sacrifice."

Pastor Russ paused slightly as he looked at the faces of those in attendance. "Every day we answer the challenge of Jesus and His cross. How we live our lives shouts our answer back to God. No one can escape the shadow of Jesus' cross. Father God looks on and does not miss anything. He takes what Jesus did very seriously and is watching to see if we also take it seriously.

It doesn't matter who you are. You might have wealth, or have little or no money. You could live in the nicest city on Earth, or you could be from Timbuktu; it doesn't matter. You need Jesus in your life, and you need to make a public confession of your faith. Don't hesitate or put it off until another day. If you sense God stirring you on the inside, come here now and make Jesus the Lord of your life." Ray was one of the first to reach the front.

Paula and Darren stared, speechless. Tears streamed down Paula's face, overcome as she was by the wonder and complexity of what she was witnessing. Darren was holding back, but inside he too knew he was witnessing something extraordinary.

There was Ray, arms uplifted, saying the sinner's prayer with another dozen or so souls who were ready to get things right with God. He walked into the service and was presented the pure and simple gospel of Jesus Christ. Now, as Darren and Paula watched, Ray was in the middle of his own personal salvation experience.

After a few emotional moments and additional ministering by the pastor to all those at the altar, tears were evident on Ray's face. There was embracing, hugs, and laughter at the altar.

Before he dismissed the group Pastor Russ gave one further instruction. "There is one very important thing you must do to be the success God intends. This thing will transform your life. The Bible tells us to, *"seek ye first the kingdom of God and His righteousness..."*, and how often, well-meaning Christians fail to do just that. Not that long ago at Freedom Church, we started to really stress the importance of beginning each and every day with prayer and time in the Word of God. This is one of the main reasons for the incredible stories and testimonies that have resulted. Start today and commit to develop the habit of spending the first moments of the day with the Lord. This will change your whole future. It doesn't matter if you start with just 5 minutes each day. Just commit to it, then do it, and you'll be forever the better for it."

When things started settling down, an elderly woman approached Ray and started speaking softly to him. Ray locked onto her and began sobbing, even though he was trying to maintain his composure. The more she spoke, the more control he lost, until he had fallen to his knees.

"Do you think this is for real? Do you think he really realizes what he's doing?" Darren asked Paula.

Still teary-eyed, Paula answered, "All I know is the Word of God says that whoever confesses with his mouth that Jesus is Lord, and believes in his heart that God raised Him from the dead, he will be saved. And that no one can declare that Jesus is Lord expect by the Holy Spirit. Well, something drew him up there, and I know deep

152

inside that it was the Holy Spirit of the living God." Darren had nothing more to say.

About forty-five minutes later they left the revival tent. Ray was still a little woozy but was regaining control. He went from giddy to introspective and back to excited. His shaky English was interspersed with words of his own world. Darren and Paula didn't understand the words, but they both sensed his joy. "Tell later, can't talk now tell later," said Ray as he rode in the back seat, taking deep breaths and laughing every now and then.

When they got back to the RV the whole group assembled, and Ray tried to explain. It took about an hour. In his home world, there were people they called "the believers." His parents were "believers," but he always thought it was a sign of weakness to believe in ancient prophets and prophecies about God. Ray started putting it all together the night before in the RV. Inspired by the part of the sermon he heard, he had started searching the Internet for information about religious history and the different religions on Earth.

He was skeptical at first, but one event got his attention. Before Ranar scientists had reached out into space, they knew that one of the stars they wanted to explore in hopes of finding other life was ours. Centuries before Ray was born, and long before they were even close to being able to travel through space, ancient astronomers of Ranar searched the stars that they one day hoped to reach.

As they looked at Earth's solar system, an unusual occurrence took place that secured our solar system on their "first to explore" list. In his research, Ray was able to match that unusual occurrence with a documented historical event on Earth.

What Ray told the group next stunned everyone present. The Ranar astronomers it turns out, had observed an intriguing, unexplainable dimming of our sun's light, followed by a restoration to its original brightness. In Ray's time, distance, and speed of light calculations, Ray was able to determine that the dimming of our sun coincided with the time that Jesus was crucified on the cross. That revelation had a profound impact on every believer present though no one said a word.

Ray said that was why he wanted to go back to the tent revival, but he was not prepared for what happened there. Ray reminded the group that in both services, Pastor Russ said that it didn't matter if you had no parents and were from Timbuktu, you needed Jesus. This hit Ray like lightning. The son of adoptive parents, he grew up in the Ranar city of Tambaktoo. When Ray heard "Timbuktu" twice which sounded so much like the name of his own home town, he felt God was talking to him.

When Ray got to this part of an already overwhelming story, he broke down again as he tried to continue. Pulling himself together, Ray was determined to finish. As overwhelming as the service had been - - hearing the name of his town and getting tear-drenched saved - - Ray had been floored by the next incident that occurred there.

The elderly woman who had spoken to him had been speaking in a language unfamiliar to her. Ray however, understood her completely. She spoke in the clear and unmistakable language of Ray's world.

God used the woman to speak intimately to Ray, even in the local dialect of his own home town. Ray broke down several times as he tried to share what God had told him through her in that intimate moment. He was not able to explain it all, but part of it was about God's love for Ray and the great plan he had for his life.

After lots of tears and laughter, the group was exhausted. This night Ray was the first one asleep. Upon awakening the next morning, Ray felt as if he'd never before had such a restful night's sleep. The peace of God which surpasses all understanding, had taken up residence.

Chapter 14

Truth or Coincidence

The next morning, Kurt left early for an appointment. Darren and Paula arrived at the house shortly before ten. They went around back to see if Ray was stirring. When several knocks failed to muster any response, Paula tried the door. It was not locked, so they entered while calling out for what they thought would be a sleepy Ray finally hearing their calls. There was no Ray in the RV. They checked outside and searched the house itself. They checked with Rene and the kids, but still no Ray.

Darren and Paula cruised the neighborhood. It was a fairly nice residential area bordered by a sizeable mall, but to no avail. About two stressful hours, a happy-go-lucky Ray returned to the frazzled waiting group sitting on the back patio of the house. The relief of Ray's safe return extinguished the apprehension of his absence, almost.

"Hey big guy, where have you been?" asked Darren rising to meet him.

"Just went see."

"To see what?" Paula asked.

"People" was the less-than-informative reply. As Darren was pulling up a chair for Ray, he said, "No problem, why don't you sit with us for a little bit and tell us how it went?"

His mood was drastically different than it had been the night before. Ray baffled the crew with, "Ray need rest now."

He turned, walked over to the RV, opened the door and went in. This left the stunned group staring at the closed RV door.

"That went well," commented Rene.

Sarcastically, Paula agreed, "Yeah, I thought so too. It's really nice that we know where he's been and what he was doing."

For the next several hours, they gave Ray some space. Kurt's absence rendered them unable to monitor Ray's computer activity. Whether Ray was sleeping or surfing remained unknown to them. What they did know was that Ray didn't seem to be interested in earthly camaraderie for the moment.

158

When Kurt returned that afternoon, the humans held a bit of a strategy meeting in the house. Kurt got on his office computer and checked the RV computer's activity. Ray wasn't sleeping, but he was getting quite proficient with computer technology. Amazingly, he was able to use the computer's keyboard to write in what had to be his own language. How he got the conversion accomplished would have been of great interest to the military fanatics obsessed with the coming invasion.

Nevertheless, it was happening right there in Kurt and Rene's RV. Uneasiness and apprehension began growing within the group of non-aliens huddled in Kurt's office. Ray was searching history, religion, politics, versions of the Bible, and alarmingly, quite a bit about the earth's history of war and violence.

Finally, Darren asked the question. "Are we all OK with this? Or am I the only one that's a little concerned here?" They were all starting to feel a little uncomfortable. Even though there was a growing concern about Ray's true intentions, they were not, as yet, ready to make any kind of call to the authorities. Were it ever to get to that point, they would be hard-pressed to even know who to call.

Ray emerged around dinnertime and seemed closer to his normal, carefree self. He was "Hungry to eat soon." Everyone set aside their concerns and enjoyed a friendly evening together, staying close to the house.

The big hit of the night was the Scripture fortune cookies Rene found at the Christian bookstore. They all got a big kick out of reading their fortunes - - eventually even Ray, who was a little puzzled at first about the whole fortune cookie thing. After some explaining, he caught on.

Ray opened one, ate the cookie, and then handed the message to Rene to read. *"Though your beginning was small, yet your latter end would increase abundantly.—* Job 8:7." There was a puzzled look on his face as he pondered what the verse meant, but that did not stop him from stuffing several more of the cookies into his pockets.

Obviously, Ray had been spending some time watching TV, from the question he asked next: "Do all buffalos fly?"

Paula repeated the question to make sure she was hearing it correctly. "Do all buffalos fly? Is that what you're asking Ray?"

Using his expanding communication skills, he nodded in the affirmative. The rest of the group looked at one another to see if anyone else understood the question. Not a clue.

Then Rene eased in, "Uh, Ray, I don't quite know how to answer that, why are you asking?"

"Me want eat buffalo wings!" Realizing what had happened, smiles broke out and Kurt explained the whole buffalo wing thing. Earlier than what seemed appropriate, Ray feigned another "tired, need to sleep" exit.

As Ray returned to the RV, the group went into monitoring mode back in Kurt's office - - more religion, more Bible, and more war. That uneasy feeling was resurfacing. Before they all started to frazzle, Darren suggested they call it a night and regroup in the morning. It seemed like there was little else to do, thus the party disbanded.

While on their way to the motel, Darren and Paula received the third, and what seemed would be the last call they would receive from Stan on one of the prepaid phones. Darren raised the phone to his ear and mostly listened. Not only was Stan concerned about coming under scrutiny, but also the search had refocused to the general area in the southern part of the state.

Since the far-reaching leads across the globe came up empty, the government was re-intensifying its focus around Arizona and New Mexico. They were closing in. Stan warned them that even using the prepaid cell phones was not foolproof and that it was not impossible for the government to make the connection. Using the phones too often might be like sending a written invitation for them to be checked out.

The stress in Stan's voice was apparent. What he was going through, and from the sound of it what he could soon be going through, was very troubling. With no real signoff, Stan was gone and the connection went dead.

Darren placed the phone back in the plastic bag. He didn't know which way to jump. First order of business in the morning would be to tell the rest of the team that they needed to come up with a real plan 'A', since without one they would likely soon be located and caught. Jerking him back from pondering all the negative possibilities he was considering, was the voice of his intended future bride.

"Everything all right?" asked Paula.

"Oh, just Stan saying that things are getting a little intense at the base. Sounds like they might be getting closer to linking him to Ray's disappearance," Darren answered.

"That is definitely not good news," said Paula. Then she asked the question that was weighing heavily on her mind. "Well, are you starting to believe, just a little? Not about aliens or the invasion, but about God?"

Darren answered as honestly as he could. "You know, I think I kind of believe, but I just don't really believe in all that fire and brimstone stuff. It seems to me that any God who would make all this wouldn't have to resort to intimidating us into believing. I think more like, if you're basically a good person, God wouldn't keep you out of heaven." Darren shrugged. "That's just the way I see it."

"Yeah, that's close to what I used to think, but that was before I started reading the Bible. The more time I spent in church and talking to serious Christians, the more I started to see God a little differently. I saw a great God who started to become envied by one of the powerful angels He had created, the devil. Satan told the angels 'you don't have to do what God says, you can do what you want to do', and many of the angels liked the sound of that. Because of the angel's free will to choose, there was a great divide in heaven. A third of the angels who liked what the devil said were cast down from heaven and from the power and positions they had been given by God."

Paula looked and paused to make sure Darren was still with her.

"I'm listening," Darren confirmed.

"And the devil still uses the same basic temptation to lead us away from God. It's always a version of 'you don't have to listen to God, you can do what you want to do,' and people like the sound of that. And, to a certain extent, that is true. We can choose to not serve God and live just doing what we want and ignoring God's intended purpose for our existence. But in so doing, we forfeit living in the peace and presence of God for all eternity, and suffer the same fate as the angels who turned from God. You still with me?"

"I understand what you're saying, but I'm still struggling with it, I mean all of it together," Darren answered.

Paula pushed on. "You have to realize that God is working to resolve the rebellion/pride issue in both the physical realm, our tangible universe, and the spiritual realm. And He's doing it in and through one single source, the sacrificial work of Jesus Christ. You see, the way God has it worked out; He has forever crushed the pride issue. We'll never be able to pat ourselves on the back in heaven about what we did or what we accomplished to get there. It will always be about what Christ did when He humbled himself and took the punishment for our rebellion, for our selfishness, for our sin.

"When I think about how Jesus willingly allowed himself to be slowly tortured to death for my selfish, prideful rebellion, I am compelled to turn from my selfish ways and serve Him the best that I can. Now, truthfully, there's not a day that goes by that I don't mess up, one way or another. Big shock, I know. But when I think about what Jesus did for me, all my petty excuses fade away and all I can say is, 'Yes, Lord.'"

Paula was about to rest her case but had one more important thought she wanted to implant in Darren's mind. "There is a scripture in the Bible that describes the 'peace of God which passes all understanding.' If there is anything I've learned about the difference between genuine believers and all those who have not found Jesus, it's this. Believers have that peace that passes all understanding, and those who have not truly accepted Jesus, do not have that peace."

She had said a lot and wanted to lighten up a little before she pushed him away. "I know it's a lot to think about, but it's something we all need to sort out. I still hope and pray that you'll soon begin to believe these things in order that we can pursue the things of God together. But it is not something I can do for you. We must all work out our salvation with God individually. Then we who are saved are to begin serving God by helping others come to a saving knowledge of Christ. We declare and demonstrate the change that has taken place within us by the words we speak and the things we do. If we are truly 'saved' there is a difference between what we used to say and do, and what we as Christians now say and do"

As she was talking, she reached over to turn up the radio and catch a little of the on-the-hour news headlines.

The female voice of the newscaster filled the SUV, "...full support of the Palestinians, as well as leaders throughout the Arab world, are well pleased with the peace accord scheduled to be signed at the end of the month in Jerusalem. The U.S. president, the prime minister of England, and several other world leaders are expected at the signing. Though some factions of the Israeli government expressed concern about the agree. . ."

Just then, an oncoming car trying to pass another car appeared over a hill. The glare of the oncoming headlights, coupled with Darren's attention on their conversation, caught Darren slightly off guard. Before he could react, the right front tire of Darren's SUV blew out, and his vehicle was pulled hard to the right and off onto the shoulder. It was all Darren could do to hold his vehicle straight and keep it from rolling.

As soon as Darren's SUV was off the highway, the two oncoming vehicles (taking both lanes) passed by going the other direction. The vehicle doing the reckless passing came within a foot of Darren's vehicle as Darren struggled to bring his vehicle to a stop on the shoulder. It all happened so fast that there were no "Look out" screams or shouts of any kind. Neither Paula nor Darren said anything for several seconds.

Finally, Paula broke the silence. "Thank You, Lord. - - - Thank You, Lord. - - - Thank You, Lord."

"Amen, and amen, and amen," agreed Darren.

As they got out of the vehicle and started changing the tire, Darren thought of another danger avoided, the stiff arm that knocked him to his knees the other day just outside the Channel 8 station. Darren wondered if the stiff arm that kept him out of that intersection and the blowout that pulled them off the highway onto the safety of the shoulder, were more than just coincidence.

"You know, the way all that just happened, I don't think we would have made it if this tire hadn't blown out when it did," he said. Darren looked at Paula and added, "Uh, perhaps I need to rethink this believing thing. Some strange things have been happening. You know what? There's another something I forgot to tell you about. I didn't even think about it until right now. I guess it was all the excitement, but remember the other day when that accident happened right in front of the station? Well, I was walking - - whoa! - - It was the same day that the light show started! And - - - "

Chapter 15

Love Letter

The following morning they arrived at Kurt's house very early. They wanted to check out the surrounding area to make sure that no government vehicles were encroaching. They did not see any suspicious governmental activity, but they did see some startling alien activity. Several blocks from the RV and walking briskly toward a strip mall was Ray. He did not detect their presence, so they followed at a safe distance.

What they witnessed relieved most of the suspicions that had been building. Ray entered the Sunrise Donut Shop, walked up to the counter and bought some donuts. Obviously Ray had a sweet tooth, and from the size of the box he walked out with, it seemed that about a dozen donuts would do the trick. Not wanting to infringe on the outing, Darren brought the SUV back to the house by a different route. They parked and waited. When Ray finally returned, no box or donuts were in sight. Paula just shook her head and smiled.

She leaned and whispered to Darren, "Invasion of the 'Donut Snatchers' sounds a little more appropriate."

When Rene asked Ray where he'd been, he responded in classic Ray style. "Ray need special food. Ray feel better now."

Rene decided to leave the children with her Aunt Margaret for the next few days, since it seemed that things were on the verge of escalating. Ray and the other adults went to the cover of the RV where Darren brought them up to speed on Stan's last call. As they brainstormed on what to do next, Ray spoke up. "Ray tell what need do now." The group was instantly quiet. "Lady at tent tell Ray what Ray need do."

Then Ray began telling the group what he felt he was supposed to do. He told them that when the elderly lady at the revival tent spoke to him he remembered something of the old prophecies that his parents believed. The Ranar prophet's spoke of the last days and how a messenger would go into the vast wilderness, return, and bring the final revelation of God.

In the span of two of their lunar cycles, or a period of about three Earth months, after receiving this final revelation, all the people of his world would choose whom they would serve. Then, even though the exact day and hour that the end-times would come could not be known, according to their ancient prophecies, their end-of-days would surely come. All the inhabitants of Ranar would choose whether or not they would serve the God of this final revelation. At this end of their time, God would return and take away those who chose to be with Him for eternity. Those who rejected Him and this final revelation would be forever rejected by Him.

Ray removed something from the top drawer of Kurt's desk as he spoke. He went on to say that the words spoken by the elderly woman at the revival were the words of God directly to him. Though he spent all his life apart from the "believer way" of his parents, he now realized that his parents were right in their belief, and that he was the messenger spoken of in the ancient Ranar prophecies.

Kurt recognized some of the computer components Ray held in his hands. They were parts Ray had scavenged from the stock of computer parts for Kurt's computer business.

Ray apologized for taking the parts. "Ray feel bad to take from Kurt computer pieces and ask Kurt forgive Ray." Ray said he felt God put them there for him to use. He added that he needed to get back to his spacecraft. Ray said that he had translated most all of the New Testament and key scriptures of the Old Testament from the Bible into his home world language. With the computer parts, he had rigged a crude interface that would connect to the computer on board the craft.

He said that his craft served a secondary function in addition to space travel. The craft was also an interstellar communication device. He and his fellow project volunteers knew that there would be no return trip back to their world, but the ship was designed to transmit one powerful subspace pulse that would be picked up by specially built receptor/booster stations positioned part-way toward the target star systems. The technology was beyond what Ray could explain in detail, but it involved bending or warping the fabric of space, thereby bringing the sender (the ship) and the receptor (Ranar) in communication proximity. Rather than taking years to make the trip, the transmission, were it to work, would take only seconds.

But the massive amount of energy expended would incinerate the ship and anything or anyone close to it when it pulsed. Nevertheless, according to Ranar prophecies, Ray's world would be evangelized within the next few months after receiving this final revelation, and then the God of this revelation would come.

The immediate question on every human mind was, '*if God was coming at that time for the believers of Ray's world, would this coincide with His coming for the believers on Earth*'? Paula sensed that the end time prophecies of Ranar and Earth were divinely connected. Getting ready and staying ready for Christ's return were priorities, now more urgent than ever.

The Ranar space exploration plan was that upon the discovery of other sentient life, follow-up plans to pursue communications with the newly discovered world would be formulated and put into effect. Ray's logical mind had always been a little skeptical about whether the transmission would work at such a great distance. He knew that the message he had prepared with Kurt's computer parts was vastly different from anything Ranar scientists would imagine receiving. Based on Ray's recent encounter with God, Ray believed that if he could get the message to the ship and get it sent, God would get it to Ranar.

This was pretty weighty stuff for the small contingent of humans assembled in the RV. Darren was first to state the problem. "OK, I guess, that's all amazing, but I do see one little problem. With all the attention on Ray, we just can't waltz back onto the base, march right up to your ship, and hook up your little gadget there."

Ray stepped up, "Get Ray close - - Ray run strong. You not see how fast Ray run with no weight on Ray."

The group was clueless about how to proceed. Just how do you infiltrate a high-security military base on full alert?

After a half-hour of rambling ideas, Darren excused himself to get his briefcase out of the SUV. No one should have had any idea where they were, so the sight of Stan leaning against Darren's SUV was startling. The first thought Darren had was, *We're busted,- - - big-time busted. They must have broken Stan, and they figured out where we are.* With his heart racing, Darren kept walking toward Stan and looked around for signs of waiting SWAT teams.

Then, when Darren reached hearing distance he cautiously asked. "Stan, how in the world did you get here? Are you by yourself?"

Stan smiled and said, "Don't worry, I'm alone, and nobody knows where I am, or where we are. Oh, and how I found you? Let's just say I put a little something extra in one of those cell phones I gave you, just in case I needed to find you. It brought me right here." Darren breathed a deep sigh of relief.

"Yeah," Stan continued. "With your friend here disappearing and everything on the craft on hold, there wasn't too much for me to do. I just told them I was going stir crazy and needed to get away for a few days. I told them to put me on days off if they had to, but I needed to take a little break. I told them to call me if anything changes."

Darren escorted Stan back to their RV base of operations. He introduced Stan to Kurt and Rene. Then he began the process of bringing Stan up to speed with all that had transpired with Ray—getting saved, ancient prophecies, and all. Stan affirmed that he was also a believer, though he confessed that he had allowed his work to encroach on his relationship with God. Still, all in all, he said that the prospects of a peaceful and

177

reasonable resolution to the problem seemed near impossible. Stan brought his internal knowledge of the base and project operations into play. After discarding one plan after another, he worked on coming up with a plan that had at least some chance of success.

"As a fallback position, and before getting too far into making plans," Stan said, "just in case we get found out before we get something figured out, and we and Ray and whoever's left somehow escape capture, we should establish a regroup position. Somewhere out of the way, something easy for everyone to locate. Kurt, is there some place around here that would work for that?"

Kurt thought and said, "Yes, there is a place that might work. It's not too hard to get to, and it's easy to locate, and all things considered, still kind of remote. Did you notice the communication towers just south of the city on that high peak? Usually there are not too many people around. It has a maintenance access road off the main highway leading into it. It could work."

"Good enough, the com towers it is," Stan said. "Let's just hope it doesn't get to that."

Ray asked to see a map to familiarize himself with where he was, where the towers were, and what other landmarks were in the area. Kurt pulled out an area map and gave Ray a quick lesson on directions and how to use a compass, which Kurt gave him just in case. Ray studied the map for about a minute and then, satisfied with his understanding of the map and how to use the compass, rejoined the group.

While Stan continued to strategize, Paula and Ray decided to spend some time away from the others to talk about God. Ray had developed an incredible understanding of God through his self-imposed crash course in Christianity. He seemed to grasp what usually takes most Christians years to discern. He understood that the heart of Christianity was loving others and setting aside self-interest. He understood that putting the best interest of others before one's own interest was clearly the example Jesus set for all of His followers.

As they strolled around the backyard away from the others, Ray asked, "Why men-kind not all serve God when hear about Jesus give life on cross?" Paula tried to explain apathy and the temptation to focus on worldly things rather than things of God. Ray shook his head and gave his version of what he'd learned from the Bible. "God not want Ray to worry about small little things. God want Ray stay on big things - - the really matter big things - - about Jesus things - - the God things who matter big. Too much time waste already. Must follow big important things of God, make God big happy."

Ray asked about the relationship between Darren and Paula, and God. Paula confided that Darren was not at the same place as Paula, but that she felt hopeful that he would soon commit to serving God with the same passion she had. Ray assured her that from his observation, Day-Run had his eyes fixed on her only and that Day-Run was probably a lot closer to making a commitment than Paula thought.

To comfort her and lighten the moment, Ray retrieved one of the scripture fortune cookies he had stashed in his pocket earlier and gave it to her. She laughed as she took the slightly broken treat and opened the package. Eating the pieces, she read the scripture inside: *"Set your mind on things above, not on things on the Earth.—Colossians 3:2."* With that, Paula felt she had received God's confirming Word and the peace that comes with it.

She knew that she was right where she was supposed to be, and doing what she was supposed to do.

Once back at the RV, Ray asked Darren to come help him with something in the backyard. He wanted to get Darren alone and do some one-on-one, alien-to-human witnessing. He also wanted to play the part of Cupid, although he had no idea who Cupid was. Covering much the same ground as he had moments before with Paula, Ray initiated a conversation about God with Darren.

"Does Day-Run believe in God/Jesus long time?" asked Ray.

Taken a little off guard, Darren answered, "Oh, I guess I've believed in God in a general way for a long time, about as far back as I can remember." Ray seemed to be focusing on what Darren said. Darren continued. "It just seems that God is so big and powerful that people don't really matter all that much, comparatively speaking."

Still no response from a reflective Ray. Darren explained further. "And the Jesus thing, I have a problem with Jesus being the only way and all that - - no offense. It just seems that an all-merciful God would not keep people out of heaven just because they didn't believe in Jesus. I wish I could believe more like Paula and even you, Ray, but I'm not there yet. Maybe I never will be there. Who knows?"

Ray nodded and then finally responded, "Ray think he understand Day-Run some little part. Ray be honest with Day-Run too. Ray not believe in God or Jesus most of time Ray alive. Ray on Ranar believe what Ray do make him good and better than others who cannot do same. Ray on Ranar big hero like astronaut here. Ray believe in self, not God.

"Now Ray come to Earth and see what not see before. Ray could not see because Ray not want to see. Ray not let God control because Ray want be in control. Ray parents know what right, but Ray too proud to listen. Ray feel shame before God at church tent. Ray see first time Ray way selfish way compared to Jesus not selfish way. See Jesus give life for others - - gave life for Ray - - make Ray heart and selfish life ashamed. But God forgive Ray and love Ray.

"Love of God grab Ray and not let go. Ray understand and believe in Jesus and plan of Father God first time and not go back to old Ray. Now live for good of others like Jesus did. Only way to show God Ray say thank you for Jesus die on cross is to help others find Jesus way to God. That is only way to prove and show love back to God."

Darren weighed the words that had traveled far to reach him. He was almost persuaded to go all out for God and to believe with the same conviction and resolve that Ray clearly had. Close as he was, his desire to remain in control was strong and his feelings of unworthiness and insecurity implanted in his youth were holding him back.

He was on the fence knowing what he should do, but paralyzed by what his self-centered nature wanted to do. Finally, he spoke, as the opportunity for a breakthrough slipped away. "Yeah, I know you're probably right - - - it would make Paula happy too. I guess I'm like the people of Earth from Missouri. They say, 'I'm from Missouri, so you have to show me.' Maybe one of these days I'll finally 'get it' and get with the program."

"Ray think Day-Run close to get right soon. You right about Paul-Ah. She want Day-Run right with God too. Ray think you two be strong together when both right with God the same. Ray believe God want you two serve before Him together."

"Oh, I don't know, Ray, I feel that Paula is a little too good for me, like I really don't deserve someone as good as her. She sure doesn't deserve a knucklehead like me."

"Ray not sure what Naklhead mean, but Day-Run right about Paul-Ah be too good for Day-Run. But Ray believe God want you together so say thank you God and serve Him both one together - - all this just what Ray think - - Day-Run decide for Day-Run." Just then, Stan found them and asked them to come back to the RV.

Chapter 16

The Song Remains the Same

After everyone got settled in the RV, Stan shared a troubling call he had just received that meant he had to leave immediately. A few moments earlier, General Adams called Stan to summon him to his office. Though meetings with the general were not out of the ordinary, something felt different in the way the general sounded. He seemed a little too guarded and gave no indication about what was going on. Stan was concerned that they had realized what he was up to, but either way, he needed to face the music and return to the base ASAP.

The group had that deer-in-the-headlights look as the mastermind of whatever plan that was coming together excused himself and walked out the door.

Paula spoke first. "I feel like something just sucked all the air out of the room."

Ray seemed relatively unconcerned and added, "Stan good man and be back soon. He with us and care stronger for what God want more than what general want."

Darren was amazed at Ray's immediate confidence in God's favor. Inside he envied Ray's growing belief in God and wondered why he, who had been hearing about God for so long, was spiritually so much further behind.

Inside his vehicle, Stan did not feel as confident and assured of himself as the image he hoped he had left with the group. The call required Stan to drive faster than he would have liked to. He did not want to compromise the group, and he was concerned that the length of time it was going to take him to get back to the base might reveal something that could jeopardize their mission. It was unsettling the way the general sounded. He had never heard or seen the general act coy before. Were there other people in the room? Stan's mind raced as he tried to guess what this might be about and especially about what error he may have committed that could have placed Ray at risk.

Back at the RV, Ray and company small-talked their way through the day, as the absence of their main strategist became more apparent. They remained in the RV, concerned that a SWAT team would be breaking in the door at any minute.

When Darren's cell phone rang mid-afternoon, it was startling and sounded much louder than usual. Darren answered. "Hello. OK - - - that's good - - - OK, I'll pass it on. We'll be here." Darren clicked off and turned to the anxiously awaiting group. "Stan said everything was OK - - - said he'd be here in a little bit and catch us all up. He also said to stick close until he got here."

Fifty minutes later, Stan pulled up next to the RV. Once inside he settled into the recliner, as the anxiously waiting group assembled. Stan slowly wiped his brow and shook his head, as he seemed to be searching for a way to explain what this urgent call was all about. "That was about the strangest meeting I've ever been in. Kendall was there, as well as a couple of guys I'd never seen before. My best guess is that whoever they were, and the way the meeting went, they were somehow tied to religious politics or a liaison to the hierarchy of some religious groups or whatever." Stan paused to see how the group was reacting, but everyone was too busy listening to be reacting.

Stan moved on. "Well, as crazy as this sounds, it seems that rumors of Ray's arrival have reached elements of the upper echelon of the religious community, which in itself is no big surprise. Considering all the people involved, it's really more amazing that more about Ray hasn't gotten out. Sure, some of the tabloids have picked up on it and run some stuff that, well, actually wasn't that far off the nark. But the good thing is that they've run so much of that over the years that most people won't pay much attention.

"There is however, one other development the general also shared. It seems that Edgar Romane, the owner of *Global Gossip* - - you know, that smut tabloid - - put up a one million dollar reward for confirmation of an alien visitation here on Earth."

Stan waited for that little bombshell to register and then continued. "Anyway, while the tabloids are trying to find aliens it seems that on the other hand, the religious power brokers on our little planet are not too thrilled about a real alien visitation. They're supposedly concerned about the possible negative repercussions and the possible adverse effects to the general public. Yeah, right. You still with me?"

Everyone nodded. Kurt added, "Unfortunately."

Stan continued, "What we have here now is a partnership of sorts between the Kendall's 'dissect him' mentality group, and the religious authorities who don't want this thing to be happening at all! They want it all too just go away and leave their global power structure undisturbed and intact. The religious powers that pull the strings are outwardly acting all concerned about the public, when in reality all they are worried about is any threat to their power and position." Stan paused and let the update continue to sink in.

Stan continued, "You know, actually, it makes for some pretty interesting bedfellows of sorts, the paranoid whacko's in the military and the paranoid whacko's in the religious hierarchy. So we'd be wise to be on our guard. We need to be careful about everyone, of course, but we also need to be cautious, even from those within the religious community."

Paula thought of a scripture and shared it with the group. "You know the Bible says, 'Not everyone who says to Me, 'Lord, Lord,' shall enter the kingdom of heaven.' What we're dealing with here are people who have a 'form of godliness, but are denying the power thereof.' They are absolutely opposed to the truth and plan of God, regardless of how pious or otherwise holy they might look."

Kurt added, "You know, to be honest, the thing that irritates me to most is Romane sticking his one million dollar nose in this. Sure, the religious aspect concerns me, but not as much as the one million dollar wild card that just popped up on the table. After all, with the military and the scientific community and so on, there are a lot of people who know about Ray."

Stan addressed Kurt's concern. "I thought about that too on the way back here. Keep in mind that all those who know Ray really exist are already and have been looking for him in probably one of the biggest searches of all time. So far, with all their effort and all their resources, they haven't succeeded!"

Kurt responded, "Yeah, you're right, but one million dollars is a lot of money, and with the uncertainty and concern about the global economy, that kind of money's going to get some serious attention - - and attention is something we really don't need right now."

Darren sarcastically summed things up. "So, what I'm hearing here Stan, is that we need to be on special guard from anyone appearing to be tied to the religious hierarchy, as well as everyone else on the planet?"

Stan nodding agreement, and in appreciation of Darren's intended humor added, "Yeah, I guess that pretty well sums it up. As long as we stay away from those two groups, we'll probably be OK."

As the team pondered these latest updates, Ray got back on the computer. He asked the group for help in understanding something he had come across while he studied earth's history. They watched as Ray started bringing up pictures of the Holocaust. Bulldozers pushing piles of emaciated bodies into mass, open graves. Videos of Jews being stripped and marched into the ovens. Terrorist bombings and airplanes crashing into buildings. Scene after scene of humanity at its worst. After bringing these images to the screen, Ray looked back over his shoulder at the group with a questioning look on his face that asked, "How do you explain this?"

Paula sighed, and then started to tell the story. As she spoke, she opened a window into the darker side of humanity. She explained the scattering of Israel over the centuries and their reemergence as a nation coming out of the ashes of World War II. She said that deep-seated anti-Semitic hatred existed throughout history and was brought to a fever pitch in World War II.

Paula referenced the Old Testament and the story of God's chosen people, Israel. They were in a continual struggle with nearly every other nation. She told the story of David and Goliath typifying the battle of God's people against the people of the world. She said that this anti-Israel/anti-God's people sentiment continues to exist to the present day. In fact, the dominant issue on the planet centered on this centuries-old conflict. She explained that this relentless hatred for the Jews was spiritually motivated and perpetuated. She said that it was born of Satan's hatred for God's chosen people, through which Jesus entered the world. Satan wanted to undermine all of God's prophecies regarding the Jews by exterminating them if he could.

Ray seemed satisfied with the explanation, though he was obviously still troubled by it. For the remainder of the evening he was reflectively quiet until he excused himself and disappeared into the privacy of the RV bedroom to "go sleep now".

Chapter 17

Reinforcements

The next morning Stan had some ideas and needed more information. Crammed back in the RV, Stan asked Ray how much time he needed to transfer and initiate the pulse signal. Ray said that the ship was DNA coded, meaning that it would automatically unlock when he made physical contact with the hull. This amazed Stan, because he knew that some of the best minds in the scientific community had tried a number of methods to breach the surface but were unsuccessful. Efforts to gain access were later halted when orders came down to cease all attempts to open the ship for fear of triggering a bigger problem.

Ray said that once the ship released its security perimeter and went into standby, all that needed to be done to effect transfer and pulse emulation was to touch the hull with the interface device he had fabricated. The integrated hull/onboard computer network would be able to read the data from the device and would automatically trigger the pulse sequence.

Stan then asked, "So then, breaking it down, how long do you need to keep the device in contact with the hull, how long for the system to load, and then how long for the pulse to actually transmit?"

Ray thought for a minute and then answered, "Identify Ray - - three Earth seconds - - read device data. Format ready send—ten Earth seconds - - transmit pulse - - - five Earth seconds."

"So, under twenty seconds, is that right?" asked Stan.

Ray responded, "Twenty Earth seconds, shorter than."

Stan rose up with a glint of hope rising in his demeanor. "All right, - - all right then, maybe, with a lot of luck - - let me think - - shift change - - a good diversion, right paperwork - - right vehicles - - get Adams to ease up a little. OK. We might be able to get you to the ship, but for how long before they intervene, there's no telling. Might be five seconds, might be fifty."

Now Stan talked very directly to Ray. "But Ray, I can pretty well tell you, there's a better chance that regardless of how close or how far you get, and especially the way it's going to seem to them, they're going try to kill you as soon as they figure out what's going on."

Everyone was quiet.

"Ray no fear die. Ray know he must try do."

Stan responded and tried to smile as restrained tears could be detected in the corners of his eyes. "I know, - - I know, - - I kind of suspected you might say something like that."

Then Stan mildly scolded himself, "I can't believe we're getting ready to do what we're getting ready to do, and I'm the one planning this thing!"

For the better part of the night Stan worked on his laptop, nearly burned up Kurt's printer, and made several phone calls. He worked late into the night and slept on the couch in the RV. The next morning Ray's movement in the RV awakened him. Stan didn't look like he had slept much. He rose quickly, started working on breakfast, and then went out to his vehicle to get a change of clothes out of his vehicle to put on after the shower he planned to take in the RV. The remainder of group was starting to arrive at the RV to hear the next step.

They were all puzzled by the interior damage to the ceiling of the RV in the kitchen area. The ceiling was smashed upwards, and parts of insulation material were hanging down in places. Kurt and Darren examined the damage and were baffled as to what had happened. Ray was curiously quiet. Soon Stan returned from his clothes run and was likewise puzzled since the RV was undamaged just a few minutes earlier.

Finally, Ray sheepishly admitted he had something to do with the damage. Before Stan left the RV, he had placed some bread in the toaster, which he forgot about, and headed out to his vehicle. While Ray was standing alone in the kitchen area, the toast popped up, and so did a very startled Ray, resulting in the damage to the ceiling. Ray was obviously embarrassed as the investigation revealed his all-too-human fear of sudden and startling things.

Kurt reached over and pulled the toaster toward Ray and said, "You mean this little thing scared you Ray?" Ray stepped back, as if he thought the thing might pop up again.

Darren said, "That's amazing. Ray's probably stronger than all of us combined, and he's afraid of a toaster!"

Kurt agreed, "Yeah, he probably wouldn't be afraid of meeting a bear in the woods, which is a good thing, right? I mean, unless the bear pulled out a toaster." Everyone laughed except Ray who was still a little red-cheeked and keeping a careful eye on that toaster.

Stan told the crew that it would probably take another day or so for him to get everything ready. Ray said that he would, "like go again fair tent place." Though no one was overly thrilled about the risk and the exposure, Darren and Kurt stepped forward to be his chaperones for this excursion back into public. Rene and Paula went off to visit the children at Aunt Margaret's. Stan got on his laptop, and Kurt, Darren, and Ray headed for the Freedom Church revival down at the fairgrounds.

When they got there mid-morning, no service was in progress. A sign out front read, "Revival Healing Service Tonight - 7 p.m." Darren and Kurt turned to leave, but Ray went inside anyway. Tidying up from the night before with broom in hand was none other than Pastor Russ himself. Seeing the pastor busy with cleaning up, Kurt excused their intrusion and again turned to leave.

The pastor immediately laid down his cleaning gear and said, "Oh no, gentlemen, I was just finishing up. Come in and have a seat. Now tell me, how can I be of service?" They drew a few chairs together to form a rough circle and sat there looking at one another.

Darren stumbled out with a few words, not knowing quite what or how much to say, especially considering the huge religious caveat from the day before. "We visited the other night, and Ray here, the big guy, was really touched. And we - - he - - wanted to come again, to visit, and uh…"

Ray broke in. "Ray feel God here strong - - - Want feel Him strong again soon."

Darren thought they would at most be joining in some Bible study already in progress and could inconspicuously ease away after Ray got his religion fix. He had no idea what to do or say next.

After a short pause Ray sensed the tongue-tied impasse they were at and broke rank. "He man of God, I know. I feel inside. OK tell him. He help us."

Yielding to the growing momentum of the Ray crusade, Darren threw his hands up and said sarcastically, "Why not? It's not like its any big deal or anything!" Taking the lead and giving Darren a chance to relax, Kurt told the story to the intently listening man of God. Once finished, they waited for the pastor's reaction.

In the same upbeat tone, demeanor and words, the pastor responded as he had thirty minutes before. "OK then, now tell me, how can I be of service?"

Kurt replied, "Well, pastor, I'm not exactly sure, but a little more of God's team on this can't hurt. And the way things have been working, we're not here by accident you know. This is, after all, where Ray got saved."

The pastor excused himself and made arrangements for his associate pastor to take the pulpit for the service that evening, explaining that something had come up. He told the associate that he wasn't sure how long he might be tied up, but that he would be in touch.

Leaving the fairgrounds with their new "Ray team" member on board, Kurt commented, "You know, my mother always said to be careful because you never know about those people you find hanging around carnivals. Look at the group here leaving the carnival fairgrounds to go off and try to save the universe - - - a reporter, a pastor, a computer programmer - - - and an alien. Just goes to show you, maybe mama knew what she was talking about."

***

Back at the base, Kendall had just gotten off the phone with the White House. He was attempting to convince the president that until T-1 was captured or killed, the ship could be used as bait, and if need be, the place where the alien scouting mission would end. Kendall wanted authorization to place a low-yield nuclear weapon near the ship with local remote triggering capability. Were T-1 to somehow regain access to the ship, the device could be detonated and the ship, T-1, and anyone anywhere near the site would be incinerated.

With the election only a few months away, the president wrestled with which course of action to take. Would it be easier to explain a nuclear accident on a military base, or face the political ramifications of allowing an alien to escape on his watch? Kendall volunteered to manage the panic trigger and was willing to make the ultimate sacrifice if necessary. If it actually came to that, the president reasoned, placing the blame on terrorists would not be all that difficult. With little evidence to prove otherwise, the president figured it was a win-win scenario. Stop or catch the alien was a win; blow it all up and blame the terrorists was a win.

Twenty minutes after Kendall made his pitch, his cell phone rang. The Secretary of Defense informed him that authorization had been given and that the order to deliver the weapon had been issued. Within twelve hours the device would be delivered, installed, armed, and ready to detonate. Kendall would be authorized to use the weapon if it was deemed necessary to preserve national security. Due to the sensitive nature of this aspect of the mission, the only base personnel aware of the device were Kendall, his immediate team, General Adams and the members of the delivery/install team.

Curry Rock Ranch, New Mexico

A hundred miles north of Albuquerque on a secluded high-plains ranch, another plan was nearing completion. Drawing on the resources of diverse operatives already in place, Ahmed and his team were preparing for the final phase of the plan that he and his brother Fahad had initiated eight months earlier from the other side of the globe.

The components of a portable, moderately powerful bomb had successfully eluded United States border security and were on American soil. The bomb was already assembled and waiting to be picked up by the terrorist chosen to deliver it to its intended target. Its destructive capability was designed to accomplish its task relying more on proximity to its target than on its explosive potential.

Their plan was designed around highly classified information obtained from high ranking sources imbedded deep within the United States government machine. Guided by the information obtained and confident of the element of surprise, the terrorist expectation of success was high. Their many months of careful preparation and positioning were as yet undetected and U.S. counter-terrorist forces were not closing in.

Chapter 18

The Great Escape

Stan was attacking his project with a vengeance when the group returned. Pastor Russ was more formally introduced to the rest of the crew. Since Stan was buried in making phone calls and fabricating computer misinformation, the others in the group decided to make one last trip into town. Ray, Paula, Darren, Kurt, Rene, and Pastor Russ jumped into the SUV. They headed for the new mall not far from the house. Darren played with the engagement ring in his pocket. He didn't have any real plan, but since the surreal adventure was escalating, he wanted to be ready to ask Paula to marry him if any reasonable opportunity arose.

As they drove, Pastor Russ asked Ray, "Just out of curiosity Ray, what was your name back on your home planet - - were you given a formal name when you were born?"

"Ray did get what call form-al name from parents but not use much. Parents like and give Ray Ranar name 'Ana-key-toes Ash-kan-az-a,' which they tell me mean like 'make father proud.'"

"I'll have to remember that," the pastor said as he made some notes and sounded out what Ray had said. They arrived at the mall, parked, and began walking through the mall, drinking in the different scenes of everyday life throughout the facility.

After ice cream and some samples from the candy store, they started to make their way back toward the parking lot. They had to pass by the mall's theater entrance where a large crowd was forming. The line to buy tickets was starting to jam things up. Though many families and children were present, a slightly rougher group of older teens and young adults were there for some of the more violent movies that were playing.

Making their way in the close quarters that the crowd was creating was becoming more and more difficult. Partway through the congested area, Ray stumbled into one of the rougher-looking youths, presumably the leader of a likewise rough-looking gang. Playing up Ray's misstep, the muscular and athletic-looking leader of the gang fast-footed and mocked Ray's reserved nature. Playing to his friends, he gave Ray the "Are you looking at me?" routine.

Ray had no idea what was going on and just stood there. The leader's gang was eating it up, as their champion made Ray look foolish. The leader suddenly gave Ray a shove to push him out of his way. Ray didn't push very easily, a lesson that Kurt knew well from the pushing contest he had with Ray a few days earlier. Still, Ray was a quick learner and responded as he thought he should, since he had learned this game with Kurt. Ray thrust his hands forward and against the leader's chest, which sent him into his gang of followers, knocking half of them down in the process. Kurt, sensing the potential danger should things escalate, hurried Ray and the group away from the gang and toward the parking lot.

They had just about made a clean getaway when one gang member saw them. The gang regrouped and was on a mission to find this dude who had the audacity to stand up to their hero. Ray and company had almost reached the SUV when the gang caught up with them. They snarled insults and encircled the SUV. Paula and Rene got into the vehicle while the guys turned and faced the angry gang. The gang continued to press closer, focusing their attention on Ray.

Standing next to Ray was Pastor Russ who wasn't wearing anything that would give away his position as a pastor. When Pastor Russ stepped forward to try to bring calm to the situation, one of the gang members pulled a knife and sliced across the pastor's outstretched right arm. The pastor quickly pulled back and covered the bleeding wound with his left hand. Ray lunged at the attacker and seized his knife-wielding arm. With his other hand, Ray grabbed the knife and took it away. Ray then grabbed the assailant by the back of his belt and lifted him off the ground.

With the attacker dangling by Ray's one hand, Ray addressed the angry gang. "No more try hurt anybody!" Ray waited for their response. They were stunned by the sight of their friend suspended and held captive by their adversary's one hand. Impatient with their lack of response, Ray shook the assailant like a rag-doll for emphasis and added, "No more war fight now!" The angry group finally got it and realized that they were up against something a lot more dangerous than they imagined.

The gang leader slowly stepped forward and said, "OK, big guy, take it easy. We get the point. Now if you'll just put my little brother down we can all go home, and nobody else will get hurt." Ray looked to his friends for direction.

Kurt stepped forward. "All right, he'll put your friend down, but first - - back off. He won't hurt him, but you better back off right now. Otherwise, just trust me; you don't want to see what could happen to your friend."

Ray was up to speed with Kurt's thinking and raised the leader's younger brother even higher for emphasis. The young man just dangled there, as if his belt had been fastened to the hook of an overhead crane. In the distance, a police siren sounded.

Aware of the approaching siren, the gang leader responded, "There's no problem here. Just set him down, and we'll be gone before you know it. Sorry we bothered you."

Kurt gave Ray the nod. Ray gently released the young man, who scampered to the safety of his own kind. True to their leader's word and with the siren getting louder, the gang quickly left. Breathing a sigh of relief, Darren turned to check on the pastor, who was obviously in serious pain. The women got out of the SUV and started to help him.

Kurt took command. "No, not here! They could change their minds and come back. Let's get out of here while the getting's good." Everyone piled back into the SUV, and within minutes they were several blocks from the mall, heading toward Kurt's house.

Kurt, becoming ever more security conscious, redirected their path. "Darren, don't go to the house! Just keep on going and head out of town. Who knows who could be following? We don't need to lead them to where we live! How's the pastor doing?"

"Still bleeding. Doesn't look really bad, but the bleeding doesn't seem to want to stop. We might need to take him to a hospital," said Rene, who had been tending to the pastor.

"No hospital!" Kurt answered quickly. "Not if you want to keep Ray from getting caught! We already have way too much attention going on right now!"

"Where to?" asked Darren.

"Head for the com towers," said Kurt. "Usually there's nobody around there, and we can figure this out there."

"There's a first aid kit in the back. Maybe we can put some kind of pressure bandage on it and get the bleeding to stop," Darren said.

"I'll get it," said Paula, who started to climb into the cargo area of the SUV.

In another few minutes, they were turning off the highway onto the maintenance access road leading to the communication towers. The nearly moonless night made it darker than usual as they wound their way deeper into the property and away from the highway traffic. About a half a mile in, Darren stopped the SUV and got out of the vehicle to check on the pastor.

Rene started to remove the towel she had been holding over the wound in hopes of stopping the bleeding. As soon as she pulled the towel free, blood started to flow heavily from the wound.

"Must be deep - - he might have cut an artery," said Kurt.

"Then we go to the hospital, right?" Rene demanded.

"I'm no doctor, but it looks kind of bad to me," added Darren.

"Me know what do," said Ray. Everyone, including the pastor, turned to look at him.

"We ask God fix arm cut."

"Absolutely," Paula quickly agreed.

"All who believe strong stay close ask God together. If not believe strong, stay away from pray place so pray stay strong." The pastor, Paula, Kurt, and Ray huddled together as Rene and Darren, a little less sure of their faith, stepped slightly back.

Once everyone found their place, Ray prayed. "Father God, we ask you fix pastor arm hurt. Pastor believe Son Jesus and help others believe Son Jesus. He good man and serve you strong - - he need arm strong serve you strong - - in Jesus' name we ask fix arm and believe you want fix - - - All-men."

Paula and the pastor agreed, "Amen"

They all smiled at one another. Almost as an afterthought, they looked down at the pastor's arm. Surrounded by the bloodstained towels was a slightly different-looking arm. The bleeding had stopped. In place of the flowing blood was a scar that appeared to be several years old. The attack mark was clearly visible, but so too was the appearance of a wound that had healed naturally. The pastor felt the wound area and dragged his fingertips across the scar to make sure it didn't just look healed. After he examined the area, he realized the healing was more than skin deep. Ray noticed the amazed look on the pastor's face - - and Paula's.

"Why look with surprise face? God say he fix when ask in Jesus' name. And God do what say." The pastor and Paula burst into laughter as tears streamed down their faces. Rene and Darren, though not directly involved in the prayer, knew that they had just witnessed a miracle.

There were a few more minutes of basking in the moment when Kurt, true to form, brought the group back to task. "That's all good, but we have to get going. I feel great, too, but if you remember, we have some really big things to work out. We need to get back to the RV and see what Stan has got planned. Let's go! Let's get moving!"

Back in the SUV, Darren heard something on the radio and turned up the volume. The male voice reporting the national news filled the interior of the vehicle: "...and the president's family to visit the Albuquerque International Balloon Festival. In order to see the early-morning launch,

Air Force One will be landing sometime during the night at the Albuquerque airport."

Darren turned the volume down and said to Paula, "You know, if all this wasn't happening, we might have been covering the president at the balloon festival."

"Yeah, and in a more perfect world we would have the president bringing Ray to the festival as an honored guest," she said. "But with all this military paranoia, I don't see these two even getting close to one another in any positive sort of way. With all that's happened I'm afraid they would shoot first and ask questions later." They were only a few miles down the highway when they came to an INS checkpoint.

"Oh, great," Kurt said as they approached the line of cars waiting to be checked.

"Why stop now?" Ray asked.

Darren almost laughed as he realized the irony of the situation and tried to explain it to Ray. "They're looking for *illegal aliens.*" Were the situation not so serious, the rest of the group would have no doubt caught the irony and burst out laughing.

Turning to Ray, Kurt said, "Ray, you can't stay in the vehicle! They're looking for IDs - - - which you don't have. Do you remember the map, and do you have the compass I gave you?"

"Ray have both."

"Great - - now here's what you need to do," Kurt said. "As soon as I tell you to, you need to get out of the car as quietly as you can and get away from this road. Try to get clear without drawing attention. Get into the shadows. If they do start to chase you, head north until you're sure you've lost them. Try not to draw attention. If you're sure you've given them the shake - - I mean that they're no longer following you - - make your way back south to the com tower area, and we'll try to meet up with you there. Understand?"

"Ray understand - - hide now - - no get caught - - go to tower place."

Darren handed Ray a prepaid phone that Stan had given him. He said, "Take this. I programmed our number in it so all you have to do is flip it open and press the send button - - the green one, twice. If we need to call you, and you hear it ringing, just press the green button once to answer it. Nobody else should be calling you, so if someone else does, just hang up - - I mean disengage by pressing end, the red button. Understand?"

"No get caught and press green button hello - - red button stop talk."

Kurt was just about at a stop when he told Ray, "OK, Ray, it's time to go." With that, Ray eased the rear door open, got out, and quietly closed the door. The remaining occupants of the vehicle were just about to breathe a sigh of relief when whistles started blowing, and INS vehicles went rushing past them. They watched Ray running down the line of cars away from the checkpoint.

Sensing their pursuit, yet not wanting to reveal his abnormal physical abilities, he ran at what he thought would be about the top speed of a human on foot. He had no idea what an impression he was making on those in pursuit. Because of the number of agents, they were closing in on his attempt to escape. It was then that Ray made an abrupt lunge perpendicular to the highway. He sprinted straight away from the road at a little over forty miles an hour and kept it up for several minutes. He was nearly three miles away from where he had left the highway and where the INS agents were concentrating their search.

He appeared to have jumped into hiding just off the road, and that was where they were focusing their search. Agents with infrared night-vision glasses scanned the countryside close to the highway but detected no movement. Choppers in the vicinity were called in, but by the time they got there Ray was eight miles away and heading north. For the time being, he had evaded capture, but the INS was continuing to expand their search.

When Ray got another fifteen miles further north, he stopped to catch his breath and watch to see if anybody or anything was following him. For five minutes he watched - - - nothing. He planned to resume his northward track and surveyed the path ahead. In the valley before him he saw some activity. He hadn't noticed it before, because he was focusing on the direction from which he'd come. His northward track would take him close to where he detected the activity, so he proceeded with caution. Though he could have given more leeway to the activity, curiosity drew him closer. When he was about fifty yards away, he could see what was going on, and he stopped to watch.

It was the scene of another INS team rounding up a group of a dozen or so illegal immigrants. They were being roughly treated and jammed into the back of an INS cargo truck. Ray didn't like what he saw and was torn by the temptation to intervene and the logic of avoiding contact. He made a few strides tracking wide of the roundup and turned to watch a little more. About then, one of the immigrants, not moving fast enough for his captors, was struck by an INS agent. Ray could feel a heated anger stirring. It seemed that the disdain he had for bullies was not limited to his home world. When the agent shoved the immigrant again, forcing him to the ground, Ray could not stand by and watch any longer.

Before he let his emotions further engulf him, and as he made his way toward the INS cargo truck, Ray spoke out loud to God. "God help Ray - - help Ray help people hurt by guard people - - don't let Ray hurt guard men bad, just help people they try hurt."

When Ray reached the nearest INS agent, who never saw him coming, he grabbed him, spun him around as if he was throwing a human discus and using centrifugal force, hurled him into another agent. When their bodies collided both agents suffered the kind of impact that could be expected from a moderate, but not life-threatening traffic accident. One agent's arm was broken, and the other's shoulder was dislocated.

Neither one was in the mood to try to stop Ray - - - nor were they capable of doing so. Ray quickly grabbed agent number three, who had just noticed the collision of agents one and two, and likewise hurled him into agent number four. The resulting broken ribs and concussions that resulted incapacitated both of them. Luckily no one was killed or fatally injured, but none of the four was in any condition to harass anyone.

Ray released the occupants of the transport truck and said," Mean men no feel mean no more. OK, you go home now." With that, Ray ran off toward the north. Another few miles, and Ray remembered the cell phone in his pocket. On the crest of the next hill Ray stopped and made the call.

This time Stan answered. "Hello Ray. This is Stan. Are you all right?"

"Ray all right, - - Ray OK."

"Where are you, Ray?"

"Ray went far north way Kurt say."

"Are they still after you?" asked Stan.

"First soldier men, no - - - other soldier men, come soon."

Stan thought for a minute, then questioned further. "Are you a good ways north?"

"Ray an hour run hard north, not close city now."

"Maybe that's good. If you could do a small something to get some attention around where you are without getting caught, and then make your way back to the towers, that would put them tracking you north and away from us. Do you think you could do something close to where you are to draw attention?"

"Ray think already do something draw attention - - - Ray start go south now. Ray be by tower in hour or close by." Click.

Chapter 19

The Flaw in the Fabric

This time Kurt, Darren, and Pastor Russ went to escort Ray back to the relative safety of the RV. Compared with the events that had already transpired, picking up Ray at the tower site was uneventful - - - at first.

After Ray was in the vehicle, Ray asked the pastor a question. "Why men here want hurt other men? Men by movie place that hurt you no respect even to God."

Pastor Russ explained, "I'm sorry to say man has had a long history of treating one another badly. It's part of man's prideful nature. The men at the mall tonight who attacked us did not know I was a pastor - - and maybe that wouldn't have made a difference. Usually in our society, a recognized representative of God is given some respect for his position, but there was nothing in the way I was dressed or looked that would have alerted them to me being a pastor."

"And that still does not excuse what the guy with the knife did," Kurt added. "It's a good thing Ray was there to intervene."

"On Ranar law no allow those mean people to others by nice people. If not get along - - - Ranar law put mean ones live away from nice people—in place not so nice live - - - like Earth prison place."

"The problems of man are well-known to God," Pastor Russ said. "And He knows that peace would not come from laws or prisons alone. He knew that the only way for people to change is from the inside out, from their hearts. A prison and strict laws can offer some measure of protection for what you call the 'nice people,' but unless the heart, the inner-being of a person is changed, peace is very fragile and easily disrupted."

"Ray no like mean bully kind of people on Ranar, and no like mean bully kind on Earth." Ray thoughtfully chose his next words. "Ray must control how he feel angry, even to bully people. Jesus not hurt back to even bully people who hurt Him."

"You know Ray, you're right, it is important to control oneself and not to over-react to things done to us," Pastor Russ said. "But we are still expected to do what we know in our hearts is right".

As Ray absorbed every word, Kurt agreed. "Amen!"

Ray summarized his understanding of God's master plan, "So God plan is God find - save us. Make us want tell others about Son Jesus. Others we tell want find new others tell about Jesus. Make us happy to do. Make God happy to see."

"Exactly!" Pastor Russ answered.

Darren stopped at Kurt's favorite travel stop on the outskirts of the city. While he was fueling up, Pastor Russ and Ray wandered around the merchandise area of the travel stop. Ray was looking at all the different items on the shelves. He noticed Pastor Russ initiating a conversation with a man who looked as if he was in his mid-forties. Curious, Ray moved closer to hear what they were talking about.

Pastor Russ, sensing the leading of the Holy Spirit said to the man. "Hey, you doing alright?" The man, who seemed to have been lost in thought, diverted his attention to the pastor.

Pastor Russ continued, "Is everything OK?"

The man responded, "Yeah, I guess so, all things considered."

The pastor continued, "Well, I guess the big question is, ah, what's your name?" Pastor Russ was speaking with authority and yet with humility.

"Andy" the man a bit cautiously yet willingly answered.

"I'm Russ. It's nice to meet you Andy. I guess the really big question is, 'Are you serving God all out like you know you should?" - - - Is He really the Lord of your life?"

Andy pondered the question, and then soberly and honestly answered. "Not really."

Pastor Russ continued. "Well, Andy you know the story about Jesus - - - how He lived and died so that we could have our sins forgiven and live with God in heaven?"

"Yeah, sure, I've been hearing that story since I was a kid"

"The truth is, Andy, we can marry the wrong person, buy the wrong car, choose the wrong job - - - but if we don't get the God – Jesus thing straight in our lives - - - nothing else really matters.

"Now Andy, if you were one of the younger kids we try to reach at our church I would tell you something that I often say to them, and that is *'God's a partying dude – He's throwing the biggest party in the history of creation and if you don't come to respect and accept what Jesus did on the cross, you don't get to go.'* – Without getting way into what spending all eternity separated from God is like, just know that you don't want to spend forever regretting not having gotten things right with Jesus.

"So Andy, a lot of time if we're honest, we come to a place where we know we should turn to God and accept Jesus, even though we aren't quite sure if we're ready yet, or how to go about it. We at least know that we should. Is that kind of where you are right now?" The pastor waited for Andy's response.

Andy did not immediately answer as he thoughtfully considered the question, and then finally said. "Yeah, pretty much - - - at least I know I should,"

Wasting no time the pastor continued as Ray watched and listened carefully. "Well, when people get to the point of knowing they should get things right with God, what I do is say a little prayer with them. First though, I tell them the prayer ahead of time so they're not worrying about what they might be agreeing to. OK? Just listen and see what you think. It goes like this, *'Dear God in heaven — I come to you in Jesus' name — I admit I have sinned — as all have sinned — I ask your forgiveness — I believe Jesus shed His blood for my sin — and gave His life that I might have eternal life — Right now I accept Jesus Christ — as the Lord and master of my life — And with your help, Lord — I purpose in my heart — to serve You from this day forward — In Jesus' name, — Amen.'"

Pastor Russ paused for a second and then asked, "How'd that sound? OK?"

Andy slowly started to nod in agreement and then said, "Yeah, that sounded pretty good."

Not missing a beat, Pastor Russ said, "OK then, well, how about we pray right now?" Andy thoughtfully replied, "Yes, - - - I mean - - - I know I need to do this - - - I'm ready."

The pastor placed his hand on Andy's shoulder, and went through the same prayer he had said a moment earlier, phrase by phrase. Andy, eyes closed and in focused agreement, repeated every word. Ray was amazed at how smoothly and easily Pastor Russ led Andy to the Lord.

Pastor Russ followed up by telling Andy that one of the first things he needed to do was to tell others about "getting saved" or "getting things right with God" or "deciding to serve the Lord" or to use whatever terminology Andy was comfortable with. It was important to start telling others about the decision he had made.

He then told Andy that he needed to start reading the Bible and to pray or talk to God daily. He next told Andy he needed to keep the company of like-minded believers, and stay away from old friends or influences that would pull him away from God.

The pastor warned Andy about how the devil would try to convince Andy that he wasn't really saved. He told Andy that the devil revisits everyone and whispers lies about not really being saved. The devil tries to tell all of us that since we still have some sinful thoughts, we aren't really saved.

The pastor explained that those kinds of thoughts are normal attacks of the devil. He described how the devil would try to steal away the purpose and godly influence that God had planned for Andy and all the other people in Andy's life. He told Andy that the church's job was to teach, lead, and encourage Andy. Then he would be able to first help others come to a saving knowledge of Christ, and then secondly a serving knowledge of Christ.

Pastor Russ and Andy exchanged phone numbers. The pastor detailed the importance of being in a Bible-teaching church every Sunday, and immediately getting involved in the things of God.

In just a few minutes Ray had seen first-hand the gospel preached one-on-one, someone say a prayer of salvation and the process of discipleship beginning. The pastor told Andy that within him was a great ministry. He told Andy he needed to trust and pursue God who would unfold the adventure of the great Christian life that had been planned for him.

Witnessing Andy getting saved rekindled the memory of Ray's salvation experience just a few days earlier. He looked away, embarrassed that someone might notice the tears welling up in his eyes.

Inside the travel stop, Darren had sensed what was going on between the pastor and Andy, but he was also watching something else. Their business concluded, the group returned to the vehicle. Darren started the vehicle, but then said, "You guys just sit here for a minute. I'm checking something out." He got out of the vehicle and walked over to the gas pump area. He milled around as he monitored the activity back in the convenience store.

Darren was troubled by a comment he heard as he and his companions were leaving the store. There was a bit of a traffic jam at the door. Ahmed and his two terrorist cousins were ready to enter the store when an overly exited group of high-school age teenagers stormed their way in front of Ahmed and his men. When the jam at the convenience door occurred, Darren heard one of Ahmed's men mumble something in Arabic toward the rambunctious teens that concerned him. Drawing on the knowledge of Arabic he had picked up during his reporting stint in the Middle East, Darren thought he heard something like,

"You won't be so happy tomorrow when your president is dead!"

Stunned, Darren sat on the information as he tried to sort it out. From his vantage point Darren kept an eye on the men in the store that he feared might be terrorists. He tried to figure out how to alert the authorities without compromising their mission to re-access Ray's ship. His mind raced as he tried to remain calm and make sure that he wasn't imagining things. Darren cautiously watched from the outside as the possible terrorists waited in line to check out. It seemed as if it was taking forever.

Pastor Russ and Ray were oblivious to Darren's concerns and continued their conversation. Pastor Russ explained that the way he led Andy to making a profession of faith was the same process he used to train the members of the congregation. The pastor was giving them the template and path with which to lead others to Jesus, no matter where they happened to be.

The pastor said a sense of urgency was moving throughout the prophetic Christian community concerning the soon return of Jesus. The escalating economic instability that was shaking the world, and all the end-time prophesied biblical events surrounding Israel, were on the one hand confirmation for believers who were looking for Jesus' return. On the other, these signs were a call-to-arms to all believers to get ready for the greatest revival the world would ever see. The shaking and turbulent times would help break the world's hold on people. This would help prepare those who were willing to really accept Jesus as their Savior.

All members were taught to memorize the same sinner's prayer Pastor Russ used with Andy, and to pre-tell it to people before actually praying with them. This would help eliminate the apprehension that people sometimes feel when someone tells them to repeat what they are about to say and would allow the people to actually focus on the prayer as they repeated the words.

He told the congregation that they needed to be "field ready" to do their part to help bring in this great end-time harvest. They needed to know how to lead someone to the Lord and then quickly bring that person up to speed so that he or she in turn could lead others to Christ. A "won by one" strategy was instilled in the members as the core mindset to fulfill their purpose as disciples of Jesus. In much the same way that a brushfire quickly spreads, the pastor was encouraging believers to spread the story of Jesus to all who would listen, in what precious little time was left.

Meanwhile, Darren was still carefully monitoring the suspected terrorists as they made their way closer to the cashier. His heart was racing as he tried to notice all the details about them that he could. Darren watched as the Middle Eastern men placed their selections on the counter and paid for them. They left the store and Darren got back into his SUV at the same time the suspected terrorist entered their vehicle. Their black Land Rover began to leave the parking lot as Darren placed his SUV in gear to follow.

Darren could remain silent no longer and alerted his companions to his concern. "Look, I hate to interrupt right now, but something is going on. When we were leaving the store I believe I heard one of the guys in the vehicle ahead saying something about the president being dead in the morning!"

He now had their full attention. He continued. "My Arabic is not the best, granted, but I'm sure I heard the words *president, dead, and morning.* You remember that the president is flying into the Albuquerque airport tonight! He could be flying in any moment, and these guys have something planned. I can feel it!"

Darren maintained a safe distance for fear of being noticed. Before long the suspected terrorists' black SUV pulled into the dimly lit parking lot of a mechanic shop about three blocks from the back side of the airport. They pulled up to the mechanic's metal frame building. All three men got out and entered the shop. Darren pulled over about a half-block away and killed the lights of his vehicle.

After watching for about a minute, Darren saw the overhead door of the mechanic shop open and a small panel truck bearing airport vehicle markings back out of the shop. Darren watched through his small high-tech binoculars. He could see that the same men had changed clothes and were wearing the authentic looking, slightly stained overalls of airport runway workers. As the third man closed the overhead door, Darren slipped his vehicle into gear and began slowly rolling toward the mechanic shop.

His heart was racing; he wasn't exactly sure what to do. Hesitating only as long as necessary, he waited until the panel truck was almost a block away and pulled up next to the Land Rover. He told Kurt to keep an eye on the truck as he jumped out to try to find anything that might help them figure out what the men might be up to.

Using his flashlight, he looked through the window and around the interior of the Land Rover. On the passenger side floor, Darren could see an operating manual for a late model jet-powered helicopter. In seconds Darren was back in his vehicle and back on the trail of the panel truck.

Kurt still had an eye on the slow-moving vehicle, and in a short time they were cautiously closing the gap. Abruptly the truck turned into the General Aviation security gate and in no time was waved through. That looked suspicious; Darren was sure gate personnel were in on the plan, whatever it was. No sense trying to enter there and alerting the terrorist to their presence.

With the clock ticking and plausible options extremely limited, Darren turned to Ray and gave him a crash course on the situation. "Look Ray, the men in the truck that just went through the gate are bad men. Remember the bad men who crashed airplanes into those two tall buildings?"

"Yes, Ray see two planes fly crash in two buildings."

"OK, Ray," Darren responded. "That's good. Well, you see these men are part of the same group, and they want to hurt more innocent people. I believe they are going to try to fly a helicopter. Do you know what a helicopter is?"

"Ray know hello-copter fly up down way."

"Good again, Ray," continued Darren. "I don't know exactly what I'm telling or asking you to do, but somehow we have to stop those men from what they are up to. I believe they are going to try to use a helicopter to crash into the president's plane or get close enough to it and explode a bomb or maybe somehow shoot the president's plane down. They'll probably come out at the last minute, right when the president's plane touches down, before anyone even sees them coming. We can't get through the gate. Before we even get a chance to explain all this, the president could be dead!"

Darren realized that only a few moments before, Ray had been feeling bad for getting physical with the INS agents, and now he was being asked to injure or possibly even cause the death of someone Ray didn't even know.

Darren needed to help Ray feel the urgency magnitude of the situation. "Remember when we talked about World War II and all the killing? Do you remember the story of David and Goliath from the Bible?"

"Ray read how bad man Goliath stand up and say mean things to God's people—and God make David strong to cut off head of bully man Goliath."

"OK, well these men are the descendants of Goliath's people, the Philistines! And they want to kill the leader of America using a helicopter," Darren said.

Ray thought for a second. "Ray no like Goliath bully and no like his bully people try to kill leader of Earth people. Ray not all way understand bully people plan but try to stop!"

Ray started to leave the vehicle when Kurt added, "Whatever happens, stop them or not, meet us back at that convenience store as soon as you get done. We still have to get you back to your ship." Ray nodded in the affirmative, jumped out of the vehicle, and in a few strides jumped over the fifteen-foot-high security fence surrounding the airport. Darren was already on one of the untraceable prepaid cell phones to try to warn of the impending terrorist plot. Hopefully, either Ray or the United States military would intervene in time.

Five miles out and on final approach, Air Force One was cleared to land. Outside a General Aviation hangar and also ready to take off, was a Euro-copter EC120B. On board was the carefully smuggled mid-sized bomb designed to do considerable damage to an in-flight Air force One. In less than two minutes the helicopter would be in sudden and dangerous proximity to Air Force One.

Ahmed's two assistants, both trained pilots, manned the helicopter as Ahmed waited just inside the hangar to watch the carnage. He never saw Ray coming from behind him. The automatic pistol he held in his hand did little good as he found himself abruptly thrown twenty feet into one of the hangar wall support beams. Following his painful impact, he slumped, semiconscious, to the cold concrete of the hangar floor.

Ahmed watched helplessly as Ray grabbed a short length of heavy-duty rope off the wall and tied it to the handle of a twenty-ton hydraulic jack weighing over thirty pounds. As the helicopter was rising and powering up to make its run, Ray began moving hurriedly in the direction of the departing aircraft. As the speed of the craft increased, Ray realized his only shot at hitting the craft was to hurl the hydraulic jack in hopes of damaging the craft. He began swinging the hydraulic jack, hanging by the rope about a foot off his right hand, in an increasingly faster sling-like circular motion. He quickly calculated his anticipated throw toward the now distancing helicopter. He was about fifty feet from the helicopter, which was now ten feet off the ground and steadily rising. Ray made one last purposeful swing and then let go of the rope.

Though Ray had targeted the center mass of the craft, he did not hit exactly where he intended. The jack smashed, seemingly without much effect, into the rear fuselage of the aircraft. Ray watched as the helicopter banked slightly and toward the runway—where the fast-approaching lights of Air force One were now clearly visible. Over Ahmed's radio, which was now lying on the floor, the pilot of the helicopter called to Ahmed, "Something hit us! Something hit us! We can still fly...we are going on - - hard to steer - - "

Chapter 20

A Late-Night Snack

Darren's call for help sounded the alarm, but by the time the message was relayed to the president's plane, it was too late to do any good. Air Force One, flaps down and helpless, lumbered toward the runway. From out of nowhere the assassin helicopter crossed its path.

The terrorists' plan had worked. They were right where they wanted to be, but there was a problem. In fact, there was a serious problem. That hydraulic jack had done considerable damage to the helicopter's ability to maneuver. Though he tried to hold position, Ahmed's cousin was unable to control the craft, which pulled him past where he wanted to be. Fight as he did, it was to no avail. By the time he triggered the bomb, the chopper had already drifted past the point where it could do significant damage to Air Force One. Air Force One's pilots saw the explosion to the left as they flew by and smoothly landed on the runway. At nearly the same time that they touched down, flight control directed Air Force One to abort, too late to matter.

From the road that circled the airport, Darren, Kurt, and Pastor Russ watched the explosion. They also saw that Air Force One was intact. Whether Ray, antiterrorist troops, homeland security, or airport personnel were responsible for saving the president didn't really matter. Knowing that evil, at least this day did not prevail, was a guarded comfort.

When they got back to the convenience store Ray was already there waiting for them. Soon they were back at the RV, and the whole team assembled to hear the Air Force One story. What Ray was embarrassed and a little reluctant to tell them was about his parting words with Ahmed after the explosion. After having verified the safety of the president's plane, Ray went back to Ahmed and vented his anger. He shouted at Ahmed, "Ray glad David cut off you family Goliath head! - - - Wish he here to cut you head off too! Ray not hurt you because Jesus say not hurt you - - - you not hurt God's people no more!"

With his venting concluded, Ray had bounded away and headed for the convenience store leaving a bewildered Ahmed to consider what he'd just seen and heard.

"It's a shame that Ray and the president can't meet. It just seems so unfair," Paula said.

Rene jumped in. "I think that with all that's happened, we might be able to contact the right people and get things worked out. Surely they would be a little more cooperative, considering that Ray just saved the president of the United States! And then we wouldn't have to worry about some SWAT team out of nowhere jumping all over us!"

"I understand, but you have to remember, the mission to reach Ray's ship is vastly more important," Kurt answered. "It's way too risky to trust the military machine and mindset."

"Well, let's at least consider it," Rene sternly countered.

The escalating friction between the spouses with their differing ideas was apparent to everyone in the RV.

Darren had an idea. "OK, let's not be hasty. Turn on the TV and let's see if making contact right now might be a little better received, considering like Rene said, that Ray did just save the president."

Kurt remained composed and turned on the TV. Switching channels, he found a news team covering the Air Force One story. He quickly turned up the volume. What they heard extinguished any hope that Ray's heroic act would result in any kind of positive relationship between the alien and the U.S. government.

The news report covered the "remarkable" story of the successful U.S. anti-terrorist effort to thwart an assassination attempt on the president. A somewhat delusional Arab terrorist, Ahmed Hussen Ali was in custody, and the other known co-conspirators were reportedly killed in the conflict.

Depending on how the "reach the ship" plan went the world would probably never know the truth about the terrorist attack. Without the intervention of a visitor to Earth from millions of miles away, the president of the United States would likely be injured or killed, and the world would again be gripped by fear, anger, and chaos.

"From the looks of how the government's already taking credit, it's obviously better to focus all attention on the task ahead," Kurt soberly continued. "Uh, Stan, just what is the plan, anyway?"

Rene, faced with the reality that the government was taking all the credit, restrained herself and realigned her focus back to the plan, whatever it was.

Stan thought before he answered. "When you can't fool them with foot work, it's time to dazzle them with - - well - - whatever else might work." It was a good thing that Stan was highly organized and detail-oriented. He would need both those qualities to implement the plan which involved official-looking but forged documents, incendiary devices, handcuffs, magnetic door placards, three rented black Suburbans, - - very standard Government Issue. All the players on the mission had and would wear matching, cool-looking FBI style shades. The plan also required one helicopter for show that Stan acquired by calling in a favor.

Stan would drive Suburban number one with Darren in the front seat and Ray in fake handcuffs in the rear. Paula would drive Suburban two, with Pastor Russ seated next to her to help sell the "task force momentum" image that Stan was trying to generate. Kurt was to drive Suburban number three, with Rene seated next to him for the same reason as Suburban number two. Stan laid out the rest of the plan. Everyone among them could see how fragile and time sensitive the plan was. When he was done, there were no supportive comments like "Good!" or "That should work!" It was quiet for several seconds as the group searched for some positive comment to make.

Then Stan finally said. "OK, I know it's a little weak, but it's the only thing I can come up with that'll get us close to that ship," Stan said, breaking the silence. "I'm counting on the orders I made up, and a couple of phone calls I've got lined up, to come through. That should give us a small window. I even think Ray's little airport visit tonight might work to our advantage. I wouldn't doubt that by now all the terrorist response groups are starting to bump into each other north of Albuquerque and that might give us the kind of distraction we need.

"The only other wrinkle that troubles me is this guy Kendall. He's messed with me on some other stuff in the past, and he's the one pushing the invasion retaliation plan. If he were to break his leg and was out of the loop on this one, I'd breathe a little easier."

Ray softly admonished Stan. "Stan, no be mad at Kendall guy, he just not know he do wrong.

God say love him anyway too. Ray want good for everybody. Ray want no hurt to no body, not right way how believer should live."

Then Ray revisited his anger and weakness in his altercation with the INS agents and also with Ahmed in the hangar. "Ray know how want hurt sometimes like Ray did with men tonight. Ray sorry to God for let mad make Ray almost hurt kill men and terror bad man - - - ask God now forgive Ray selfish act mad - - - ask you forgive Ray how get mad too." The group reassured Ray that all was forgiven, and Ray felt the weight of his burdened conscience begin to lift from him.

There were a few questions about the plan, but in the end, Ray put his stamp of approval on it. "Plan good plan. Believe God like plan. God help make plan work." With all in agreement and the time established, Stan suggested they get some sleep.

***

Ray had been looking out onto the driveway through a narrow gap left by the RV shade. It seemed that someone in the driveway was trying to see what was going on inside the RV. Ray slowly got up and told the group he was going outside.

"Ray see someone try see inside at us - - stay same and keep talk same. I go see who look at us."

With that, Ray was out the door and closing in on the figure in the driveway. Ray's sudden exit and speed caught the intruder off guard. The intruder's first thought was to protect the camcorder he had been using, but that impulse left him no time to react to the fast-approaching Ray. The intruder lowered the camcorder and turned to run, but it was too late. Ray wrapped his arm around the intruder's waist and seized the camcorder with his left hand. As his captive protested and tried to scream, Ray tightened his arm around the intruder's waist and squeezed just enough air out of him so there was no way he could scream for help. Ray quickly looked to see if anyone was watching. Then he turned and quickly trotted off with the trespasser firmly in his grasp.

With minimal effort, Ray entered the RV and dropped Kurt's teenage neighbor on the floor, right in the middle of the stunned group. As the boy struggled to regain his breath, Ray, camcorder still in hand said, "He look take picture at us with this. Ray grab him and picture thing. Bring here now see what should do now?"

With that, Ray handed the camcorder to Kurt.

The boy was still trying to regain his breath and his composure when Kurt realized he recognized him. "Billy - - Billy MacDowell - - is that you?"

The boy mustered a weak "Yes, sir, Mr. Kurt. I didn't mean any harm. I was just playing with my camcorder, and this guy just grabbed me."

"At 1 o'clock in the morning?" Kurt challenged.

Billy thought for a second. "Uh, yeah, uh, I was trying out the night-vision function, and uh - - - "

But Kurt had been examining the camcorder, and he knew better. "That's funny. The camcorder is still running, and the night-vision function isn't even on. And let me see here, when I rewind it a little bit - - there we go - - play. Let's see, it looks like you were trying to see what we are doing in here."

"So, Billy, care to tell us what this is all about?" Kurt asked sternly.

Billy had apparently recovered from his ride in Ray's grip, because now he was feisty and defensive. "Hey, you can't hold me here like this, and that guy can't just grab me the way he did! I want to call my parents - - or no, the police - - right now!"

Something didn't feel right, and Kurt wasn't budging. "First off, it seems to me you were trespassing and recording us without our knowledge or permission. And about calling your parents, maybe that's a good idea. Give me your cell phone, now!"

Intimidated by Kurt's anger, Billy handed over his cell phone. Kurt took the phone and got up to leave the RV. Billy protested. "Hey, what about calling my parents?"

"In due time. You just stay here and keep quiet. I'll be back in a few minutes, and then we'll decide about reuniting you with your folks."

Several uncomfortable minutes passed inside the RV. No one spoke. Then Kurt opened the door to the RV and asked Ray, Darren, Stan and the pastor to join him outside. The women were to keep an eye on Billy for a few more minutes.

With the guys assembled outside, Kurt wasted little time and spoke softly but with urgency. "I didn't call his folks, but I did do a little checking on his phone activity - - Seems he placed a call to a New York number - - to the office of the *Global Gossip*!"

"Well, that's great," Darren said. "So what's the plan now? We can interrogate him, but we can't really trust what he might say. Maybe it's too late already."

"No, we don't know that," Stan said. "We'll need to interrogate him, and right, we can't assume that what he tells us is the truth, but maybe we can discern something, anything that helps us figure out how to move forward."

"We've got a safe-room, panic-room, bomb-shelter kind of room off of our basement," Kurt offered. "It's probably a good place to take him for a little chat. It's soundproof and sealed off from everything."

Darren agreed. "That'll work."

Billy was escorted, primarily by Ray, to the underground shelter and seated in a chair in the middle of the room where the questioning began. Billy was evasive and uncooperative at first, but

247

then Kurt picked up a broom that was leaning against the wall and handed it over to Ray. Ray took the broom and waited for instructions. "OK, Ray, hold the shaft with both hands," Kurt said. "Now see if you can break it."

Putting forth some effort, Ray broke the shaft with a loud snap. Then Kurt told Ray to hold Billy's forearm in the same way. Ray understood the drama they were orchestrating. He had no intention of harming the boy, but he seized the boy's arm with a firm grip.

Billy was scared. "Is he the alien?"

Coldly and deliberately, Kurt responded. "Yes, he is. And he's got no problem with tearing your arm off for a little snack."

By now, Billy was practically hyperventilating. Stan continued. "Now, we're going to ask you a few questions, and we need your answers to be immediate and honest. Otherwise, I'll tell this big alien it's OK to have a bite. Do you understand me? Don't worry. If you're honest, we won't hurt you. We'll leave you here - - locked up in this room until our business is finished. Do you understand?"

"Yes, sir," said Billy.

"OK, tell us what you were doing outside, why you were there, and who else knows what you were up to," Stan said.

Billy answered immediately. "OK, uh, I'd noticed all the activity at Kurt and Rene's, and I heard all this stuff about the alien deal, and then I heard about the reward, and I thought I'd try to get some video just in case you guys had something to do with the alien, and uh - - - "

Stan pressed him further. "So what about talking to *Global Gossip?*"

"Oh, yeah, uh, I called them to try to find out how the reward thing works - - just in case."

Kurt jumped in. "You talked to them for seven minutes! It sure doesn't take seven minutes to say that little!"

"I was on hold! I was on hold for five minutes, at least!"

Stan cut in. "So where did you tell them you were? What phone number did you give them to call you back? What name did you give them?"

"I didn't give them anything. I just asked how someone could be sure they would get the money and that someone else wouldn't steal the information and claim it for themselves. They said that if someone is really serious that they issue you a special code that identifies you and only you, and that by using that I could somehow protect myself."

"So what else did you tell them about what's going on here?" Stan asked.

"Nothing. I mean, when I called them I didn't even know for sure there was any alien around here. It's just that one million dollars is a lot of money, so I figured it was worth looking around, just in case, and this was the first place that came to mind because of the vehicles and stuff - - honest!"

Stan thought about what he'd heard and decided he needed confirmation. Stan looked at Ray. "Are you a little bit hungry, alien?" Ray, in an absolutely convincing manner said, "Yes, alien hungry and like soft human hand to eat."

Billy began sobbing. "I told the truth! I told the truth! Don't hurt me!"

Ray could no longer maintain his fierce and intimidating role and suddenly broke character. He put his arm around the boy and said, "Me no hurt boy - - no even like human hand to eat. Just want make sure boy tell truth."

Billy's other interrogators then broke and began assuring him that no harm would come to him; they were just trying to get to the truth. Billy eased up and was so relieved that he even got to the point of laughing. Kurt told Billy that he would have to stay in the shelter for the rest of the day, with no communication with the outside world. Should their mission fail, Billy would be rescued by someone the group trusted. A very relieved Billy thought that was great news. He even started to act as if he was on board with the mission. He even admitted his parents would be out of town for the next few days so his absence would pose no immediate concern.

Kurt and company made the shelter secure - - hopefully, escape proof, sealed the access, and returned to the RV to explain their plan to Paula and Rene.

Chapter 21

Plan A

The group reconvened back in the RV where Kurt explained the "Billy" game plan and the results of their interrogation of Billy. As he glanced over at Rene, he ended his update with, "So I guess a little kidnapping at this point actually makes sense."

Before Rene could restrain herself, she blurted out, "That's just great, Kurt! Billy, our own neighbor - - - jailed - - - and in our storm shelter!"

Everyone suddenly got quiet. Rene soon composed herself and continued. "I'm sorry. It just caught me off guard. I know we have to do what we have to do. You're sure he'll be all right?"

"I sure hope so. He should be, anyway," Kurt said.

Ray and Paula drifted off into the backyard to talk privately, maybe for the last time. Paula was feeling the weight of the task ahead. Ray calmed her and assured her.

"It will work good to us. God already see it work."

"I know you're right, and I know what we're doing is right, but I also know that they will try to stop us. No, let me say it right - - they will try to stop you, at all costs. They won't be waiting for an explanation. They'll be shooting first." Paula said.

Ray cut her off. "You not worry, Paul-Ah, God told what Ray should do this from woman at tent. Why God tell do if should not do? God cannot tell do what hurt you, only what good to you. Evil one devil cannot tell you do good to you, only tell bad to you. Ray decide believe God and good in God no matter what happen. God plan right plan."

The strength of his conviction helped Paula regain her peace.

Ray apologized for his inability to speak correctly. "Ray Ranar language not have many small in-between word like you language. Make hard make talk smooth. Ray try and mix up." Then Ray asked about Darren. "What plan with Day-Run now, he believe God more now?"

Paula sighed. "I hope he does. He doesn't let me in on very much, though. It's like he's afraid to

254

admit that I was right about God, and he's holding back because of his pride. Sometimes I just want to shake him and tell him "Look! - - - Even Ray, who's an alien and only been on the planet a few days 'GETS IT' (no offense to you Ray)"

Ray smiled. "God give Ray look see ahead. Ray believe Day-Run more close than Paul-Ah think. Listen what Ray think, Day-Run come hot fire for God soon. You see soon next little time." Paula let Ray's confidence continue to lift her spirits. Ray continued, "Ray see good come for Day-Run, God see too, God and he come to one."

"You're right. I'm going to start believing it and speaking it. Darren's going to be a great man of God one day - - no, a great man of God - - soon! He's going to become hungry for the Word of God. Hey, I'm starting to like talking like this!"

After returning to the RV, Ray asked Pastor Russ, "Can pastor talk Ray outside?" The pastor agreed, and soon they were outside and away from the others in the group. Ray recognized Pastor Russ's authority and knowledge, and struggled to phrase the question that was stirring within him. "Why some who say believe in Jesus not act or do like they say believe and others like you and Paul-Ah do and act like really believe?"

Pastor Russ smiled. "You are becoming quite a student of human behavior, Ray. There are some scriptures in the Bible that speak to that very question. One talks about how faith without 'works', without action, is dead. I believe this describes those who profess to believe in Jesus but don't really do anything to bring others to a saving knowledge of Jesus. They're afraid or ashamed of the story of Jesus and do not want to risk what others might think of them if they stand up for Jesus. They are more worried about what others think, than what God thinks. There is little or no fruit in their lives."

Ray looked a little perplexed over the "fruit" reference.

Pastor Russ clarified what he meant. "Sorry, Ray. The 'fruit' refers to the people whom they have helped find Jesus or encouraged in their walk with Jesus. Being a Christian is being Christ-like, loving others as Jesus did and helping others do the same. I believe if there's no desire to be fruitful for God, you could easily question whether someone is really a believer or saved at all. Maybe someone like that will just barely make it into heaven. I wonder if many who fall into this category will not make it at all. Jesus said that 'If

256

you are ashamed of me before men, I will be ashamed of you before My Father in heaven.'"

Ray quietly pondered what the pastor had said. Eventually he soberly said, "Must not stand before Father God with no fruit. Son Jesus deserve Ray and all people bring much fruit."

They returned to the RV, where everyone was taking time to digest the plan and their own part in this risky venture. Ray sensed the restlessness in the group and passed around some of the few scripture fortune cookies he had stockpiled and hidden. No one seemed in the mood to eat them right then, so they stashed them away for later. With the vehicles ready and under tarps in Kurt's backyard, the group tried to relax.

Pastor Russ also sensed the weight of their mission and the effect it was having on the team. Each member of the group needed to be at peace about their part in it. As the team gathered around, Pastor Russ began to speak. "I have to admit, these past few days got me thinking. I guess you could say my perspective has been broadened a bit. I mean, I didn't question God making everything, but to be honest, I never really thought too much about what else might be out there. I kind of thought of things in terms of our little planet being the focal point of God's attention. Now that Ray has entered the picture, I can see that my perception of God has been a little too narrow.

"I just re-read two interesting passages in scripture and both are words spoken by Christ Himself. In Matthew Jesus commands his disciples to go and make disciples of all nations, clearly referring to the confines of this world. It is there He commands that group of followers, His disciples, to carry His story to the ends of the Earth.

"Yet, in the book of John in the Bible, Jesus says 'And other sheep *I* have which are not of this fold; them also *I* must bring, and they will hear My voice; and there will be one flock and one shepherd.' I believe these 'other sheep' that Jesus said that *He must bring* includes Ray's world, and maybe even far beyond that, should God so choose."

Pastor Russ continued as everyone listened. "I have done some research and figured that sharing what I had found now would help confirm that we are where we are supposed to be, and that God is with us in this endeavor.

"I know that a month ago, none of us could ever have imagined finding ourselves here; about to embark on a mission that seems to have so little chance of success. I looked up what Ray's home-world name might mean in our languages. Ray said it was 'Ana-key-toes Ash-kan-az-a.' I found out that in Greek, and also in the biblical names and meanings, there are two words - - 'Anakletos Ashkenaz' - - which together mean *'calling forth - - a fire that spreads.'* I believe Ray's Ranar name, and the meanings I found in our ancient languages, are no accident or coincidence. I believe God planned this revelation for our little group gathered here - - - for this exact moment in time."

Ray closed his eyes as God's affirming presence enveloped him. The group also silently soaked up God's well-timed revelation.

There remained one last crucial thing to be done. Pastor Russ took the lead. "It's time to pray." With that, they all joined hands and bowed their heads. Pastor Russ raised his face toward heaven and solemnly called out to God, pausing as he spoke, *"Lord God Almighty — God of heaven and all that is — we stand before You humbled that You have brought us to this place — So very much is at stake — We know we cannot succeed without*

Your help — In the name of Your obedient Son, Jesus — we ask You to place Your hand upon our efforts — and that You protect us in His holy name — Spirit of the Living God — we ask You to guide us, and lead us, and make for us a way where there seems to be no way — Lord God, we come together in agreement — believing that Your love extends beyond what we've known — to the farthest reaches of everything that exists — and that includes Ray's home world also — We are ready to do all that we know to do — that they too might hear the words of life — that the door of eternal life through belief in Your Son, Jesus, be opened to them —— Lord, grant us favor as we give all the honor — and all the praise — and all the glory to You — In Jesus' mighty name we pray — And everyone who agrees with this says, — 'Amen,'", to which every soul present agreed, "Amen."

Chapter 22

Going All In

Three a.m. came like an Amtrak train. Having hardly slept, everybody was exhausted but up, moving and making sure they had everything they needed to do their part. Stan pulled out the bio-hazard suits, medical masks, and related paraphernalia. He instructed the team to put them on. He then affixed magnetic door signs to the doors of all three Suburbans. They were identical to the sign on the helicopter that would meet them at the gate. The signs read in big letters "CDC— Centers for Disease Control— Quarantine Unit."

The team suited up and off they went. Ray appeared to be handcuffed in the back seat of vehicle number one with his data interface device on the seat next to him. He was not wearing his weights; Darren asked how it felt to be rid of them. "Ray no like weight thing. Feel good with no belt weight hold down."

They traveled in caravan down Interstate 25 toward the base with their flashers on. Darren played with the engagement ring he'd been carrying in his pocket.

In vehicle number three, Rene said to Kurt, "You know, it's still hard to believe all this is really happening. And what makes it all the more frustrating and what still troubles me is the fact that Ray should be treated like a hero and not like some escaped convict! He did save the President of the United States last night and maybe even helped stop World War III from starting!"

"Yeah, I know - - it does seem that calling the authorities and telling them the truth could be the right thing to do. It sure seems that it would be much easier for all of us. It's almost as if it's some tantalizing option, that in actuality could easily destroy what I believe God is really trying to do here."

Rene reluctantly agreed. "I know you're right, but it's still aggravating."

In vehicle number one, Darren said, "You know one good thing, Stan?"

Stan shrugged and waited.

"Well, ever since Kurt brought up those communication towers as a place to regroup, I've been worried that I'd end up having to climb up one. Let's just say I'm not all that crazy about heights. So instead, I should be happy that now all I have to worry about is getting shot at."

Stan answered, "So, it's a good thing then, right?"

Darren was making small talk, to avoid thinking about the unresolved issue going through his mind. He was still trying to figure out whether he believed in God enough, and, maybe more importantly, was he worthy enough to be involved in all this. How did he ever find himself in this situation? Was sending a two-thousand-year-old story to another world really worth the risk they were taking?

Out of nervousness more than anything, he reached in his pocket and pulled out the last three scripture fortune cookies Ray had given him. He gave one to Stan, one to Ray and kept the last for himself. Ray tore his cookie packet open and placed the broken pieces in his mouth. Stan inhaled his fairly quickly, while Darren absently mindedly ate his.

Upon finishing his cookie, Stan read his scripture message. "Hey, listen to this one *'He made the stars also'.*—Genesis 1:16."

Darren had forgotten about the message from his cookie and saw it had fallen onto the seat. He picked it up and read the message to himself: "So will I seek out My sheep and deliver them from all the places where they were scattered.—" Ezekiel 34:12. Darren took a deep breath. He knew that God was knocking on the door to his heart, beckoning him to totally sell out to Him. He felt something deep inside that he never let himself feel before. The power of the well-timed revelation words of God accomplished the purpose God intended. Darren's concerns about his worthiness or about the worth of their mission dissolved and were gone. From that moment on, he knew that he was "all in."

Darren said a silent prayer to God and made a silent promise: "Lord, if You see us through the day, I'll go where You want me to go. I'll say what You want me to say. And I'll do what You want me to do. And Lord, with Your help, I *will* become the man that You intend for me to be, - - - and the man that Paula needs me to be. In Jesus' name, Amen."

Stan asked Ray what his fortune-cookie message said. Ray sheepishly answered, "Ray not know - - Ray forget message part and already eat cookie - - Ray eat paper too. Sorry no can tell message part." Darren and Stan couldn't help but smile and shake their heads.

Though it was never said, Stan was clearly in command of the mission. It was coming up on 5 a.m. and Stan was relieved to find that they were a little ahead of schedule. It was better to have a few minutes to spare than to be a few minutes behind.

Then, in Suburban number three, Kurt's cell phone rang. Rene listened as Kurt talked to the other party on the phone. "Yes. No, we're not. Are you sure? And just when did you get the alarm? How soon? So they should be there about now. No, no. That's fine. I understand. OK, we'll start heading that way. Thanks."

Kurt took a couple of breaths before he tried to explain things to Rene. He decided instead to call Stan to inform them both at the same time. Once Kurt got Stan on the line, he explained the reason for the call. "I just got a call from our alarm monitoring company. It seems that they got a trigger off one of the smoke alarms back at the house, one of the basement alarms! It appears that Billy may have started a fire to trigger the alarm system and get out sooner than we had planned. He's probably getting out right about now. I guess that million dollar reward overwhelmed Billy's spirit of cooperation that he was starting to show. Man, for the love of money." The mission's small window of opportunity was narrowing.

Stan then received a call-waiting signal and checked to see who it was. It was General Adams. Stan cleared his call with Kurt and took the general's call. The general had been troubled by the placement of the nuclear warhead and its activation. Since Stan had been out of the loop, the general felt compelled to bring him up to speed on this troubling development. Stan mostly listened and thanked the general before he hung up. He wrestled with what he just heard for about thirty seconds and then told the group via radio that since they were running a little ahead of schedule, he wanted everyone to pull into an upcoming rest area for an update.

Stan led the group past the main parking area and stopped at the far end, away from the other cars. He got out of his vehicle and signaled the others to park nearby.

Before the others got there, Darren asked, "What's up?'

"You'll see soon enough" replied Stan.

In another minute everyone was assembled. Stan addressed the group. "First, we're good on time so this stop won't throw us off schedule. There are a couple of new developments that I need to make you aware of. I just got two phone calls that affect our mission. First, seems Billy started a fire back at Kurt and Rene's house and triggered the smoke alarm to draw attention. The authorities are probably there now. On the other call General Adams just told me that the search for Ray was focusing on a hot lead that suggested he was being helped by a family in the Albuquerque area. The information came from a teenager who had been locked in a basement so that cat's crawled half out the bag. We can pretty well assume your neighbor Billy is telling them everything he can think of.

Stan saw the drained expression on all their faces and continued. "Now I know that sounds really bad, but actually there is a good side. The general added that the search for Ray was focusing on Albuquerque and the surrounding area. A sizeable detachment of personnel from the base is heading north toward Albuquerque to help in the search as we speak. So this is actually a good thing. The base security will be a little lighter than usual, and it might be just the break we need to make all of this work."

Stan could see that this perspective helped the group recover from the weight of his initial announcement.

After he let their spirits brighten, he got ready to tell them what really prompted the stop. "More importantly, General Adams told me that the Department of Defense has placed a live and armed nuclear weapon near the ship as a last line of defense, - - - to keep Ray from escaping or making contact with the rest of his 'army.'" Stan said sarcastically.

"As I might have imagined Kendall's right in the middle of it and is the one carrying the nuclear triggering device. He has presidential authority to detonate the device at the first sign that control of the ship is at risk. What this means is that the complexion of our mission has changed. It is no longer a question of succeed or fail, and we probably end up in jail. Now it is to succeed or fail and, well, I'm sure you get the picture." Stan waited for everyone to get the picture.

"Get Ray close as can and Ray get by ship Ray own self."

"I understand your willingness Ray, but I don't think you'll be able to get near the ship without our plan getting you past most of the initial barriers," Stan said.

Stan sensed that the team might be struggling with what they were now facing. He gave them some time to consider this ominous development. "We're still OK on time, so everybody take a minute and think about where you are in this thing."

Darren put his hand on Paula's shoulder and led her a few feet away where they could talk. "I know I have been a little slow about getting on board with this, but now I know that this mission is way more important than what I feel or like."

He put both his hands on Paula's shoulders as he faced her. The emotion in his voice started to break through, "You know, I've been planning to ask you to marry me for a good while. I was just looking for the right place and the right time. And now it looks like we may be running - - - " As he was speaking he started to bring his right knee to the ground as he presented the ring he'd carried for so long.

Paula broke in. "The answer is yes, no matter what happens today." They quickly embraced and hurriedly turned their attention back to the group.

Darren, speaking for the two of them now, said, "We're both all in."

"Well, I'm thrilled that you two finally got that straight," Stan said. "I was starting to wonder what was taking you so long, but let's just hope that we're all here to make it to the wedding."

Stan turned to Kurt and Rene. "Don't even think about it. You have two young children, and they will not grow up without their parents."

Kurt took a deep breath and started to protest.

"It's not even an option," Stan said, cutting him off. "Here's what you are going to do. As soon as we get a pass through the main gate, you are to break formation and leave the base immediately. Get as far away as you can as fast as you can, a minimum of ten miles. Understood?"

Momentarily hesitating Kurt said. "Understood. We'll clear the area ASAP."

"All right. Now we *are* starting to run short of time," Stan said. "Back in the vehicles. Time to go!"

Stan had planned their arrival for 6 a.m. to coincide with command shift change. He hoped all the other parts of the plan would come together without a hitch. He had the forged documents ready in his briefcase: signed executive order, letter from the Secretary of Defense, fabricated toxicological reports, biohazard decals, and NASA documents.

Stan commented to himself, "Yep, got em' all."

Chapter 23

In Harm's Way

About ten miles and ten minutes from the gate, Stan's cell phone rang. It was the pilot of the helicopter scheduled to meet them. Stan had called in a lot of favors he had accumulated over the years, and the chopper was a big payback. Looking off to the right, he spotted the chopper tracking them about a hundred yards out. The CDC signs on the chopper looked great in the early morning sunlight. Stan had no idea how many laws he was breaking, but he was sure there were enough criminal violations to not only end his career, but also get him incarcerated for the rest of his life. Heck, he might even get shot for treason, that is, if he lived through the next thirty minutes. The weight-filled minutes were starting to rush by.

Using the two-way radios, Stan readied the team. "OK guys, we're thirty seconds to the gate." Stan abruptly pulled up to the main gate guard station. He wanted to make it look as if they were on a serious mission and weren't there to waste any time. The helicopter swung directly to their aft position and held formation as Stan stopped at the gate. Rolling the window down as the guards came out to do the walk-around inspection, Stan started right into his spiel. Flashing the orders and documents as the chopper hovered behind them, confused things slightly, just as intended.

The photo CDC identification badges that Stan had created from everyone's driver's license looked authentic. Everyone except Ray held their IDs up to the windows for the guards to see. Stan had intentionally left his briefcase open with more official documents in plain sight, along with the yellow and black biohazard decals.

Stan pointed to Ray and spun a yarn about national security, a highly contagious radioactive virus, and the executive orders to immediately contain and quarantine the virus. Pointing back at Ray, he threw in the words "highly contagious carrier." A minute before, and as part of the plan, Ray had poured a nasty-looking greenish-yellow liquid, composed of clear syrup and food coloring, into his mouth, and drooled a little out for effect. The guard talking to Stan instinctively stepped back from the vehicle, which he now believed was carrying a highly contagious and dangerous person. The door to the plan working opened ever so slightly. The guard called in for confirmation and asked what to do.

Stan pushed. "Hurry up, soldier! We've got to get this guy inside and on life support and quarantined ASAP!" Now the phone calls that Stan had set up in advance, calls that had to be perfectly timed, came into play. A few minutes before Stan and the others reached the gate, two high-ranking NASA and military officials had called to alert base security of an imminent, radioactive virus threat and a quarantine order from the CDC. When the guard called in, the new watch commander had just been advised of a decision to raise the national threat status, related to a biological or radiological threat. He could hear Stan in the background still selling the deal to the guard. " - - - sooner we can get clear of this guy; it will be better for everybody." In his effort to respond and contain this perceived "threat" to the country, the watch commander gave the order to let them through the main gate.

With the first hurdle crossed, the two vehicles and one helicopter forged ahead toward the hangar where Ray's craft was secured. Kurt and Rene broke formation and turned back onto the highway. The rest of the team focused on the confinement hangar ahead and the second checkpoint.

It was a three-minute ride from the main gate to the hangar. Stepping it up to around sixty mph. and with the chopper pulling up the rear, the operation looked pretty genuine. The routine was pretty much the same at the hangar, and the guard there backed down and them pass through.

The vehicles stopped and parked at the hangar's entrance. The chopper veered off and away from the hangar. The pilot would keep on going and become invisible as soon as possible. He hoped he would never be linked to whatever was really going on.

Moving as a cohesive unit, the CDC team got out of their vehicles and authoritatively forced their "prisoner" , Ray, out of the vehicle. They marched him in right through the front door and past the offices located just inside. Stan had orchestrated the entire scenario, knowing that human nature usually yields to those who take charge, who seem to be in authority, and are confident about what they are doing.

Truth be known, they were flying by the seat of their pants. They had reached the point where

Stan anticipated the momentum of their bold entrance would begin to falter. It was time for the "smoke and mirrors" part of the show, Stan thought, as they cleared the office area.

Pulling up the rear and according to plan, Darren set down the tote bag he was carrying next to the water cooler on the side wall of the main office area. As he released the bag, he was careful to push the trigger button that Stan had rigged with a five-second delay. They were ten feet into the hangar when the trick bag erupted back in the office area.

Thick, heavy black smoke oozed out of the bag. No personnel or soldiers were nearby when it started which gave the smoke time to envelop the room. In seconds the source of the smoke was near impossible to determine. In a few more seconds other office personnel near the hangar entrance noticed the smoke. The smoke alarm sounded and then all hell broke loose.

They were now about a hundred yards from the tarp-walled perimeter of the craft containment area. Ray discarded the fake handcuffs and secured the interface device with his right hand. He picked up his pace a little, and was shifting from the position of the one guarded, to the one leading the group. Ray knew that anyone close to the ship when it pulsed would be in danger.

Startled by the alarm, the technicians and other personnel in the hangar started to hurriedly evacuate the building. Ray took command of the mission. He said loud enough for his team to hear, "You all stop now! Not go close by ship - - much danger close by ship! Ray got ball now!" Yielding to the stern tone coming from Ray, the team began to slow a little.

Dead ahead and walking straight toward them was Agent Kendall. From that distance, and because he was focusing on the fire alarm, Kendall did not immediately recognize the approaching group. A few steps later Kendall focused on the rapidly approaching intruders and was puzzled by what he was seeing. He hesitated. He'd been longing to get his hands on what he considered an "alien threat to the human race," and there he was, forty feet away and walking straight toward him.

A few more steps and Ray and Kendall crossed paths as Kendall was momentarily stunned and confused by the suddenness of what was happening. Another staggering step and Kendall knew something was very wrong as he struggled to regain his composure and react as he felt he should. Ray was striding away from his team and had already moved past Kendall. Seeing Ray closing in on the ship triggered Kendall's deepest fear.

Kendall called out to alert the guards stationed near the craft. "It's the alien! He's trying to get to the ship! Shoot to kill! Shoot to kill!" Screaming as loud as he could, Kendall was running back toward the craft and after Ray. "Shoot to kill!" The guards responded and started to raise their weapons. At the same time, someone turned the fire alarm off. A surreal quiet permeated the hangar.

Switching the device to his left hand, Ray grabbed the edge of a nearby table with his right hand. He twirled around like a discus thrower and hurled the table toward the two closest rifle-wielding guards. Traveling at considerable speed, the table leveled the guards before they were able to fire. Ray was fifty feet from the craft. Two more guards were coming around the ship and starting to fire at Ray.

Moving with super-human agility, Ray darted to the left and slid on the floor where the momentum of his lunge slid him over to some tables set up with electronic gear. He grabbed the bundle of wires and cables used to supply power to the equipment that curved around behind the craft. Sliding into a standing position, and with the cables tightly grasped in his right hand, Ray gave a long, hard pull on the wiring bundle. Electronic equipment on the tables went flying and crashing. The pull also caused the wires on the floor close to the soldiers to swing suddenly inward. The two armed guards were violently upended as the wires knocked their legs out from under them and sent them crashing to the floor.

Immediately Ray resumed course toward the craft. Ray's delay with the guards had helped Kendall to almost catch up with him. No rational unarmed person, having just witnessed what happened to the guards, would ever have considered trying to physically stop Ray. Kendall however, was not rational and his rage was controlling him. The CDC crew was watching from about thirty yards away, trying to heed Ray's command but also wanting to help. But so far, with his superhuman strength, speed, and agility, Ray was holding his own.

Guards from other parts of the facility were now closing in. Kendall was still hollering "Stop him! Stop him! Shoot to kill!" - - and lunged onto

Ray's back. Ray turned and tried to reach back over his shoulder with his right hand and grab hold of Kendall to pull him off. Just then the approaching soldiers began firing as they neared the scene. The CDC crew cowered as the bullets flew by. Ray finally got Kendall by the shoulder and pulled him around and in front of him. Holding him there and holding the device between them, Ray turned his back in the direction of the approaching soldiers. Though Kendall struggled to free himself, Ray firmly held him and protected him from the bullets with his own body.

A few seconds later, several of the bullets tore into Ray's back, leg, and foot. Both Kendall and the device were still protected by Ray's body. The CDC team was screaming for the shooting to stop. Some of the soldiers stopped firing, but others fired a few more rounds. One grazed the back side of Ray's head bringing Ray to his knees and Kendall to the ground with him. Finally, the shooting stopped.

Hurt badly but still conscious and determined, Ray took a deep, labored breath and swung Kendall toward the CDC team and away from the craft.

"Not go close by ship - - ship burn hot and harm to you - - I go!" he said to Kendall.

And then it happened. Kendall panicked. He grasped the nuclear trigger pendant hanging from his neck, and pushed the button. The warhead started its sixty-second countdown to detonation.

There was no way Kendall could stop the countdown once it had begun. No one moved.

Ray stood and took another deep breath. He stumbled the remaining twenty feet to the edge of the craft.

The guards started to lift their rifles again. Paula cried out, "Don't shoot! Don't shoot! He means no harm! For God's sake, don't shoot!" Weeping, she and the rest of the team began to rush toward the ship.

Taking longer and deeper breaths, Ray tried to stay focused. He was bleeding profusely. Most of his backside was drenched in blood. His lungs had been punctured by the hail of bullets. Blood was filling his lung cavity. He was drowning in his own blood. Reaching the craft, Ray leaned against the ship and pressed the device against the hull.

Thirty seconds to detonation.

Ray struggled to stay conscious and to keep the device against the hull as long as possible.

The CDC crew knew their friend was dying. There was nothing they could do.

Time froze. No one moved. No guards, no soldiers, not even Kendall. The only sound was that of Ray's struggled breathing as he fought hard for a little more time. He kept the device pressed firmly against the surface of the ship.

Ray took another deep breath, held it for a few seconds, and then slowly let it out. He never took another breath. He was gone - - - -

Ray's body rested motionless against the ship.

A few seconds later, a low tone from the ship began increasing in intensity. Several more seconds, and the ship began to glow a strange blue-green color.

Seventeen seconds to detonation.

The sound and the glow of the ship intensified. The sound was piercing. The glow turned a dazzling white.

Everyone instinctively began moving away from the ship. The intensity of the light made it impossible to look at.

Seven seconds to detonation.

Suddenly an electromagnetic pulse (EMP) emanated from the ship. It was designed by Ranar scientist to disable any power source near the ship that could interfere with its signal pulse.

At three seconds the bomb countdown clock went black. The electromagnetic pulse had done its job.

The piercing sound and dazzling light abruptly ceased.

The craft and everything near it, including Ray, had been vaporized. Everything within a ten-foot area of the craft was gone. A scorched, jagged-edge of smoldering matter lined a crater beneath the place where the craft had been suspended. Singed and severed suspension straps dangled above. The air was charged with the odor of molten metal and burnt electrical wires.

Ray's friends slowly grouped together. A dazed and bewildered Kendall slowly approached them. His expression said it all. He was struggling with the realization that the alien, the enemy that he had tried so desperately to stop, had protected him from the gunfire and the pulsing ship.

He spoke softly to the group. "T-1 saved me. Why? Why did he save *me*? He wouldn't let me go. Somebody please tell me: Why did he save me?"

No one could speak. They had just lost a precious friend. Finally, struggling to contain her pain and her emotions, Paula focused on Kendall and said. "First, Sir, his name was Ray. And I'm proud to say that he called me his friend."

Paula paused slightly as her emotion threatened to overwhelm her.

She looked in the direction of her friends and then back at Kendall. "And you probably won't understand this Sir, - - but you asked, Why did he save you? Sir, - - - - because he loved you."

Chapter 24

For the Record

White Sands, New Mexico

The events at White Sands never became widely known. The world, reeling from the effects of the global nationalization of the banking industry, moved tentatively forward through growing fears of pending economic collapse. With the increasing paralysis of world trade, America the once-blazing beacon of freedom, liberty, and hope in the world, had become the largest debtor nation on the planet. In so doing, America had relinquished its global leadership role.

America was emerging as the new subservient partner and member of the "New World Order". The power center for world policy and monetary decisions shifted from America to the Euro-Asian alliance, which included the Middle East. Every nation was keenly focused on the prospects of "world peace". The Middle East peace accord had just been signed and endorsed by Israel, the United States, and every Arab country. The mainstream media praised and reveled in this historic moment. They were condescending in

287

their attitude toward the conservatives, Christians, and many Israelis who had spoken out against this New World Order-brokered, peace accord.

As a worldwide political and social transformation was beginning, so too was an end-time worldwide revival beginning. Captivated by these historic events, most of the world had little interest in the kind of event that had happened at White Sands.

To say that the events following the incineration of the ship went smoothly or that the government officials assigned to look into the matter were understanding would be grossly inaccurate. For nearly two weeks, the remaining members of Ray's escape team were interviewed and interrogated.

Most of the grillings conducted in the first few days were done individually, with each participant in the escape plan facing several interrogators at once. Every detail that each participant divulged was compared to the details obtained from the other escape team members. The military was even able to track down the helicopter and the pilot used in the escape plan, but determined early on that the pilot had no in-depth knowledge of the plan.

Stan's military career was over - - with prejudice. He did not seem bitter or all that troubled over it. The team members were kept isolated from each other, but knowing that they had done the right thing was enough to sustain them. Their interrogators were intent on confirming what they believed to be true. They could not comprehend nor easily accept what they learned, as a result of all their questioning.

The members of this ragtag team, who were kept apart while being debriefed, told the same story. They told the story of an alien going to a tent revival, getting "saved", and convincing them to help him get back to his ship to send the salvation message back to his home world.

No matter how the interrogators asked the question, the story came back steadfast and unwavering. The alien got saved; he translated the New Testament into his home-world language, sent the message back to his home planet, and was vaporized along with the ship in the process. Aside from the fact that the government had volumes of video, audio, and massive amounts of other data, they had no ship and they had no alien.

This loss was a bitter pill to swallow. Government interrogators were having trouble with the responses they were getting from the team, especially since the team's explanation was not scientifically verifiable. The troubling consistency to their stories produced a fairly universal "deer-in-the-headlights" look on the faces of the government facilitators.

Not only did the team members corroborate the details of the plan from beginning to end, but also each team member was absolutely convinced and adamant about one more thing: that Jesus' return to Earth was imminent. The interrogators sat tongue-tied as the team members kept talking to them about Jesus and witnessing to them.

Late in the second week, the beleaguered escape team garnered a little support from an unexpected source. Since the day of the pulse transmission, Agent Kendall had been visibly affected. After wrestling with his own part in the death of Ray and the destruction of the spaceship, Kendall had a dramatic change of heart. After monitoring the testimonies of all the accomplices regarding the escape attempt, Kendall stepped up in defense of those he had once opposed. His conversion—switching from opposing the alien's friends, to supporting the team and what they had done, had an effect. Agent Kendall's animosity toward the alien had been no secret. To see him defend the team began to make a difference. His change of heart gave subtle permission to others to let up a little.

A few days later the team was miraculously released with no more than the standard warnings not to divulge anything to anyone for reasons of national security and, to be readily available if needed.

The team got busy with trying to resume "normal" life, but with a new sense of urgency. They talked about Jesus and the importance of knowing Him as the Lord and Master of one's life. Most people they talked to continued to focus on their own self-centered life, and in so doing rejected Jesus' great sacrifice. But some they talked to would stop and listen. Using Pastor Russ's salvation prayer method, a few of those made professions of faith in Jesus. They spoke the words of life and affirmed their decision to follow and serve the Lord Jesus Christ.

**

It was now three weeks since the transmission pulse. After a brief honeymoon in Hawaii, Darren and Paula returned to

Albuquerque. They wanted to see their friends one last time before attempting to resume their lives in Houston. Pastor Russ had performed the wedding ceremony eight days earlier with the entire team present.

Shortly after arriving in Albuquerque, Darren received an unexpected text message on his cell phone. The message simply read, "Com Towers - Tonight 7 p.m." Darren didn't recognize the number the message was sent from, but he knew that the only people who would send such a message were those he trusted with his life.

He and Paula (who had received the same text message), made plans to arrive at the towers a little early. They were curious but not alarmed or fearful. The only fear they had experienced lately was from the government. Since they had already been caught, interrogated and released, they looked forward to the com tower meeting with eagerness, rather than apprehension.

"Seems like it's got to be Kurt, but you never know," Said Darren.

Paula responded. "Let's just go and see. What's the worst that could happen?"

Darren and Paula turned off the main highway and onto the maintenance access road that wound its way up to the com towers. With the sun getting lower in the late afternoon sky, the diamond on Paula's ring finger directed the sun's light throughout the interior of their vehicle. She had never before seen it radiate so intensely.

Paula gazed at the display of lights dancing around in every direction. She turned to Darren as she held up the ring between them and said, "You did good "D", you did really, really good."

As they pulled up, they found Kurt, Rene, and Pastor Russ already waiting for them. A little picnic table and six folding chairs had been set up. About the time they reached the group, Stan was also just pulling up. In a few short minutes everyone exchanged hugs and took their places on the folding chairs. Kurt, who had surreptitiously sent the text messages stalled a bit, acting as if he was waiting for the person who really called the meeting to speak up.

The members of the group looked around at one another to see who would take responsibility and start explaining what was going on. After about thirty seconds of a convincing performance by Kurt, he finally confessed. "Well," he said, "I probably shouldn't keep messing with everybody, but when I thought about how you" - - he looked straight at Darren - - "used to mess with me back in school, I had to get back at you." A friendly groan rose from the group, and then a little laughter broke the ice.

"OK, you got me," Darren said. "You got all of us. So is there any real reason you called us together? Or did you think maybe a little get-together after the government's inquisition seemed appropriate? Either way, it's OK, but is there something else?"

Kurt nodded his head and reached for the laptop on the table in front of him. "I guess this comes more under something else." Kurt spun his laptop around so the screen faced the rest of the group. "Well, I don't know about the rest of you, but all that we've been through has affected my ability to get back to normal on the home front."

"That's probably true for all of us. So what's with the laptop?" Paula asked. Everyone was anxious to get to the reason for the meeting.

"Let me give you a brief intro, and then I have something for you to watch. I've seen it already. OK - - - Anyway, I was busy trying to get back into the swing of things in my business. I get this e-mail with an attachment. It had yesterday's date on it, and there was no name listed as the sender. All it had was this attachment which I very carefully opened. And well, here - - it speaks for itself. It's not very long. I've watched it several times, so just watch it for yourself."

Kurt rose to get something he said he'd been asked to bring to the group. He started the video. The group huddled together and watched the laptop come to life as Kurt set a shopping bag on the end of the table.

Suddenly, a home video of Ray filled the screen. It was shot inside the RV shortly before the group ventured out on their mission to return to the ship. Ray was a little disoriented and unsure of himself, just like humans when they make their first video. Once he was satisfied with his position on the screen and that both video and audio were running, he settled a bit, and looked directly into the camera.

"Hallow friends. Ray hope make this right and you get see and hear together OK. May be you no get see and we not even get by ship, maybe all get caught and all in big Earth prison place, maybe you no get this because Ray not smart enough to fix send so get later, but think Ray maybe smart enough find way to make work OK."

"Hope Kurt find and bring special gift Ray find. Ray want to share special Earth thing he find with you the special friends to Ray. Ray hope you like special thing Ray find. But not want you to sit long time with big happy face on face. Enjoy and like special thing OK, then time talk about more important thing. Now OK for you to have special thing. I wait some little time while Kurt show special thing to you."

With that said, the screen went black and all eyes turned to Kurt. Not hesitating, Kurt pushed the large shopping bag to the center of the table.

After a few seconds, Paula looked at Kurt, as did the others in the group. Seeing the video of Ray was an unexpected and emotional event. Drying her eyes with the heels of her hands, she asked Kurt, "So OK, what's in the bag?"

Kurt smiled, reached down, and folded down the sides of the shopping bag to reveal two white boxes. Imprinted on the top of each one was an unmistakable yellow and orange logo of the Sunrise Donut Shop.

As subdued laughter and smiles broke out, Kurt began passing chocolate glazed donuts to all in attendance. Everyone took bites and laughed together. For a few moments no one paid much attention to the paused and blank screen on the laptop.

Then, with an uncanny sense of timing, Ray came back again on screen. "Ray hope you like surprise but now Ray want to say what even now hard to say. When Ray call you friends he not say right way - - not way Ray mean really feel - - better way to say you family to Ray. Ray know big risk all you make to bring Ray back to ship. Ray know ship burn hot to send message so Ray know he not make away from ship alive, but Ray not want any you get hurt if try to help Ray get close to ship. Ray OK if Ray not make past ship burn time."

On screen Ray looked back over his shoulder as if to make sure no one had entered the RV. Satisfied he was undiscovered, Ray continued. "So you no get hurt mean much to Ray and Ray pray God put His strong protect hand on you, and believe God hear what Ray pray, and He OK with what Ray ask. Pray God to make message to get to Ranar so my Ranar people learn about Jesus truth to God way.

"Ray now tell other thing Ray afraid to tell face to face and not want you to see when time to go to ship. Right now Ray little bit scared and fear Ray not do all Ray must do on mission because fear push on Ray. Ray afraid to let you Ray friends know how Ray feels fear some little bit right now. Ray pray God help Ray fight fear so Ray do what Ray need to do to get to ship and not let you my friends down, and not let God down.

"Ray heart ache hurt when think how Ray feel to you. Ray feel love to you. You bring Ray to place where Ray find love of Jesus and Ray no can say big enough words say big enough thanks to you. Ray say thanks to you and love you for all time forever. Ray know too that not much time left to Jesus come back time.

"Ray know and pray God to help you stay strong for Him in little time left. Now time all who believe push hard to tell all others Jesus right way. Ray now understand like Apostle Paul who write much new part Bible. Ray knows one who no accept Jesus cannot go heaven and be with Jesus.

Nothing really matter but find Jesus way and serve Him.

Ray know it hard and many not listen or want to hear truth. No worry about ones who fight against you and no believe in Jesus. Tell anyway! Tell Jesus story for ones who do listen! Time to do what God wants when hear small voice of God tell us what do."

Acting as if he just heard something outside the RV, Ray turned and said, "Must need to go now!" On screen Ray looked back over his shoulder as he sensed someone at the RV door. "Ray think you here at door to leave go to ship now. Bye you now - - And hallow to you at door - - Ray feel much love you."

Ray's arm moved forward as he reached to shut down the computer he was using. The screen went black. Kurt slowly closed the laptop.

Tears welled up in every eye. No one spoke for nearly a minute as they were all individually reflecting on what they had just seen and heard. Each one present sensed the Spirit of the living God imparting a sense of urgency about the mission that lay ahead.

Trying to convince people of Ray's incredible recent visit to Earth would likely accomplish very little. It would just embroil them in controversy and waste valuable time. The real story, the one that needed to be told and believed, was the one about another visitor to Earth two thousand years ago. All else mattered very little.

Stirred by his growing faith, Darren finally was ready to step forward and take the lead. He looked around at the small group and said, "It's time to get busy."

Then, emboldened by Ray's message, the whole team rose together to join the growing number of committed believers worldwide, in the battle to reach as many as would listen, in *the precious little time left* . . . . . .

The End

"God plan is God find - save us. Make us want tell others about Son Jesus. Others we tell want find new others tell about Jesus. Make us happy to do. Make God happy to see."

— Ray

"And other sheep I have which are not of this fold; them also I must bring, and they will hear My voice; and there will be one flock and one shepherd." (John 10:16 NKJV)

— Jesus Christ